'One kiss,' he said hoarsely.

Startled, Karen was still gathering her wits as he stepped towards her and hauled her against his chest. The sensation of heat and damp from his sweater enveloped her, even as the wild fresh scent of the sea and the Atlantic air invaded her senses so profoundly that she suddenly felt dizzy as well as exhilarated.

Then, as suddenly and abruptly as he had pulled her into his arms, Gray released her.

'Are you okay?'

He voiced his concern almost grudgingly, as if he couldn't wait to be gone. Karen suddenly wanted him gone too. Now she understood why hate and love were so closely intertwined.

'Why should you care?' she tried, but was unable to prevent the sob that accompanied her words.

'I *do* care, damn you!'

Shaking her head, Karen blinked up at him through eyes that were helplessly brimming with tears. 'No, you don't. Just go. Please... just go.'

The day **Maggie Cox** saw the film version of *Wuthering Heights*, with a beautiful Merle Oberon and a very handsome Laurence Olivier, was the day she became hooked on romance. From that day onwards she spent a lot of time dreaming up her own romances, secretly hoping that one day she might become published and get paid for doing what she loved most! Now that her dream is being realised, she wakes up every morning and counts her blessings. She is married to a gorgeous man, and is the mother of two wonderful sons. Her two other great passions in life—besides her family and reading/writing—are music and films.

THE BROODING STRANGER

BY
MAGGIE COX

First published in Great Britain 2011
by Mills & Boon, an imprint of Harlequin (UK) Limited,
Eton House, 18-24 Paradise Road, Richmond, Surrey TW9 1SR

© Maggie Cox 2011

ISBN: 978 0 263 22024 7

Harlequin (UK) policy is to use papers that are natural, renewable and recyclable products and made from wood grown in sustainable forests. The logging and manufacturing process conform to the legal environmental regulations of the country of origin.

Printed and bound in Great Britain
by CPI Antony Rowe, Chippenham, Wiltshire

THE BROODING STRANGER

To the wonderful Conar and Sandy, and the equally
wonderful Luke and Mia, with my everlasting love.

CHAPTER ONE

To KAREN, the thumping tread thundering in her direction sounded like a herd of wildebeest on the rampage, and for a few vivid seconds she imagined she had somehow stumbled into some other dimension. Lord knew it couldn't be beyond the bounds of possibility in these deep, labyrinthine scented woods she'd recently taken to wandering in. A lively imagination was bound to go haywire. And right now Karen's imagination was doing just that. She regretted taking the sleeping pills she'd swallowed last night to help her drop off—especially when her head felt as though every percussion instrument in the world was being played inside it. Her wits needed to be razor-sharp—not dulled by medication of any kind.

As the thumping tread drew nearer, she glanced through the tangle of trees and foliage, fear coating her mouth as surely as if her dentist had numbed her in preparation for a filling. She couldn't run. The bones in her legs had turned to water and it was impossible to think straight. Her gaze swept down desperately to the sensible walking boots she wore that were liberally caked in mud. She told herself she could sprint if she had to—but from what? She had yet to find out. *Oh, Lord! Don't let me faint...anything but that. Please don't let me lose consciousness.* Her desperate silent plea was bordering on a mantra as she waited for whatever was coming towards her, ice-cold terror jack-knifing through her heart.

Seconds later, a fawn-coloured monster hurtled out of the trees into the clearing where Karen had turned to stone—heading with a great lolloping gait towards her. A strangled gasp left her lips as she came face to face with the unseen terror that had halted her morning walk with such spine-tingling fear, her heartbeat mimicking an increasingly loud drumroll in her ears. He was a beast and no mistake! What idiot would let such a creature loose? Left alone to roam and terrify and possibly attack at will? At the thought of the latter possibility, she made her gaze home in anxiously on the huge fawn head and wide mouth, saw the creature's long tongue, lolling and wet as he panted heavily, and felt physically sick.

A commanding shout rang out that took them both by surprise. The beast pricked up his ears as though he were a transmitter receiving a signal, and came to an abrupt stop only bare inches from her, his ears cocked, his intimidating energy streaking between them like lightning.

'Oh, God!' Karen covered her mouth with her hands and cursed the foolish tears that hazed her wide blue eyes. It was going to be all right, she told herself. The creature had an owner. Irresponsible clod he must be, but he hadn't let the beast out on its own. Thank God for small mercies.

When he appeared from out of the trees, the man appeared as shocked to see her as Karen had been at the sight of his animal—*shocked but apparently unrepentant*... That much was evident even in the space of just a few seconds. Pausing briefly to assess the situation, he immediately gave her the impression that he was the one who held the upper hand, and something told Karen that apologies or concern for another didn't come easily to him. Remorse was probably just as alien. There was something innately proud and overbearing in his lean rugged stance that immediately raised her hackles and put her senses on high alert.

Tall and unquestioningly commanding, with black hair that

edged untamed and untrimmed onto his shoulders in arrogant defiance of trend or convention, he had a hard, unforgiving face that even at a distance looked forbiddingly incapable of any notion of kindness whatsoever. Perhaps it would have been better if she *had* fainted, Karen thought wildly. Here she was, at not much past seven o'clock in the morning—despite her sleeping pills—alone in the woods with an intimidating dog and his equally intimidating owner. If only she had listened to the instincts of her tired, aching body and succumbed to an extra hour or so in bed. But, no... As usual she'd had to push herself to the limit. Past events might have taken their toll, but no one would accuse her of being lazy or idle. Maybe she'd have cause to revise that opinion later, she fretted now, her gaze fixed on the dominating individual striding towards her. She'd have to wait and see.

As he walked there was a kind of reined-in anger in his tread, and his boots were crunching through the carpet of twigs and mulch as if tolling a death knell on Karen's peace of mind. When he came to a stop just behind the animal, he reached out and roughly stroked the oversized head.

'Good boy.' He stopped petting the dog, then pushed his hand deep into the pocket of the battered leather jacket he wore, which might have been a high fashion item for the mouth-watering effect it had on that hard rangy body. Nonetheless, Karen all but shook with the effort of trying to contain her rage.

'Good boy?' she echoed in a disbelieving rasp, 'Your damn dog—if that's what he is, and I have my doubts—scared the living daylights out of me! What do you think you're doing, letting him run loose like that?'

'This is a free country. You can walk for miles in these woods without meeting a soul. Besides, Chase wouldn't hurt you...not unless I told him to.'

A glint crept into eyes that were the winter-grey of an

icy lake. Strangely light. Teamed with that rich, cultured voice, they were potent enough to cause a ripple of unease in anyone.

'Chase? That's his name? How apt. What is he, exactly?' Karen plumped for bravado to waylay the pulsing thud of fear that was rolling through her in increasingly disturbing waves.

'Great Dane.' He spat the words out as if only a fool would have to ask him that.

'Well, he still shouldn't be off the lead.' Ignoring his obvious contempt, she folded her arms defensively across her thick navy fleece, silently cursing his innately masculine ability to intimidate and belittle—and amazed by her temerity in pursuing a conversation with such a man for even a second longer than necessary. His accent was rather more clipped than the softer lilt she had became used to from the locals.

Just in front of her, Chase breathed heavily in a cloud of steam, his ears still pricked, as if waiting for the next instruction from his master. Karen kept a wary eye on him in case he should suddenly make a lunge, despite what his owner had said. Right now she trusted neither one of them.

'The problem seems to me to be strangers in the woods making a fuss over nothing.' An innate arrogance angled his jaw, highlighting the high, sculpted cheekbones and the disdainful slash of his mouth. 'Come on, Chase. It's high time we headed home.'

The dog leapt away at his master's words and Karen knew she had been dismissed—dismissed and discarded as nothing more than a trifling annoyance, a gnat on the end of his battered leather sleeve. He hadn't even offered her the most grudging apology for frightening her half out of her wits.

Okay, perhaps she'd overreacted a little at the idea of his dog being off his leash, when these woods weren't exactly overpopulated with folk out for a stroll…but even so. Her body tight with indignation, she was even more unsettled when the stranger turned back to regard her with a glance that could easily have matched the temperature in a deep freeze.

'By the way, if you're planning on coming this way tomorrow I can assure you we won't be taking this route again. We value our privacy, Chase and I.'

'Do you seriously imagine I'd want to come this way again after the fright I've just had?' Karen's chin jutted forward, her blue eyes challenging the cutting arrogance in the stranger's hostile glance, despite her desire to escape as soon as possible.

The corners of his lips curled upwards in an almost wicked caricature of a smile. Karen blanched.

'Nothing surprises me about the female species, little girl. Now, run along—and if anyone asks why you look so pale, you can tell them that you just bumped into the big bad wolf in the woods. Be thankful he didn't eat you for breakfast.' And, smiling his cold unnerving smile, he turned away.

'Very funny,' Karen murmured under her breath, but silently acknowledged it was anything *but*.

A nearby branch whinnied and creaked in the wind, almost making her jump out of her skin. Alarmed, and shaken by the anger that still lodged like a red-hot stone in her chest, she stomped off in the opposite direction from the dark, hostile stranger, furious with herself because she was crying again. Only this morning she'd promised herself that today was the day she would finally turn off the waterworks for good. Fat chance of that after that highly unpleasant little encounter!

That reference of his about the 'big bad wolf' had chilled her to the bone. Had he been referring to that beast of a dog, or himself? *Most definitely himself*, she decided, shivering, and walked on.

Back at the old stone cottage where she had hidden herself away for the past three months, she saw with satisfaction that the fire she'd started in the ancient iron grate was well underway, the peat and twigs hissing and crackling nicely. It was amazing how small, everyday things like that gave her such a sense of achievement these days. She supposed it was because she'd had to learn how to do them all by herself. The heat that started to permeate from the blaze lent some much needed warmth to the chill damp air that clung like frosted mist round the old place—that seeped into its very walls.

Sometimes it even made her clothes feel damp when she put them on in the morning. And at night it was so cold that Karen had taken to wearing both pyjamas and a dressing gown in bed. Her mother would absolutely hate such an abode. She'd probably ask just what she was trying to prove by living in such primitive conditions. Just as well, then, that she wasn't around to comment.

Shivering, Karen stripped off her rain-dampened fleece and hurriedly laid it over the back of a chair. Lighting the gas burner on the stove, she filled the slightly dented copper kettle and plunked it down with a sense of something vitally important being accomplished…*tea*. She couldn't really think until she'd imbibed at least two or three cups. This morning she was even more in need of it than usual, since that horribly frightening incident with the man in black and his beast of a dog.

Great Dane, indeed—he was more like a slavering cave troll! Just who was that hostile stranger, and where was he from? She'd been living in the area for three months now, and hadn't heard mention of him from anyone. Mrs Kennedy in the local shop was the font of all wisdom, and even she hadn't mentioned the strange well-spoken Irishman and his huge dog—at least not in Karen's hearing. Sighing, she registered the sound of the kettle whistling, and hurriedly put the makings of her tea together with a determined purpose that had definitely been absent when she'd forlornly left the house to venture into the woods.

Her fellow walker might have been unpleasant, antisocial and taciturn, but, recalling his image now, Karen wondered if his unsettling demeanour wasn't some kind of shield that cloaked some deep, personal unhappiness. Even though he'd probably not cared that both he and his dog had frightened her, the morose expression in those unusual compelling grey eyes of his had somehow haunted her. What had put it there? she wondered. Was he recovering from some terrible shock or sorrow? *Karen could relate to that.* Not least because in the past eighteen months she'd been to hell and back herself.

In fact, she was far from certain whether she'd returned yet. There were days when she was so dark in spirit that she almost couldn't face waking up in the morning. But slowly, inch by inch, she'd begun to see that the possibility of healing her wounded spirit in this beautiful place in the west of Ireland was real and not just wishful thinking. With its wild mountain backdrop, mysterious woods and the vast Atlantic Ocean only a short walk from her door, its beauty had started to penetrate the gloom that had overshadowed her since the tragedy. The wildness and isolation of her surroundings had provided a welcome sanctuary to help ease the fear and heartache that so often deluged her, and she'd learned there was a good reason why people referred to the healing powers of nature.

One day when she was whole again, she told herself, she might find the courage to go home... One day...but just not yet.

Gray O'Connell couldn't seem to get the image of the pretty blonde stranger who had lost her temper with him out of his head...*feisty little thing.* He grimaced. With every step he took on the route back to the house, her exquisite features— particularly her lovely blue eyes—became clearer and more compelling. *Who in blazes was she?* There were a few Brits in these parts who had holiday homes, but in the midst of October the homes usually stood empty and forlorn.

Then he remembered something that made him stop and shake his head with a groan. He should have kept on top of things better. Instead he'd been progressively letting things slide, he realised. *It certainly wasn't the sharp, incisive mind-set that had helped him make his fortune in London.*

Suddenly aware of who the girl might be, he wondered what made her stay here when in another month winter would bite hard, quickly replacing the mellow autumnal air and making even the local inhabitants long for summer again. Perhaps she was a loner, like him? he reflected. What if personal circumstances had driven her to take refuge here? Gray of all people could understand the need for solitude and quiet—though a fat lot of good it seemed to be doing him lately.

Not wanting to explore that particular line of thought, and irritably snapping out of his reverie, he lengthened his stride and determinedly headed for home….

'And I'll take some of that lovely soda bread, if I may, Mrs Kennedy?'

Standing on the other side of the counter from the ebullient Eileen Kennedy, Karen was in silent admiration of how such a plump, elderly woman could still be so robust and also graceful on her feet. Bustling here and there, reaching up to sturdy home-made shelves that had probably been there for ever, rooting amongst tins of fruit and packets of jelly and instant sauce mixes to supply Karen's grocery list, she kept up a steady stream of chat that was strangely comforting. The trouble was Karen had grown so used to being on her own here that there weren't many people whose company she could tolerate for long. The grandmotherly Irish woman was a definite exception.

'Now then, me darlin', is that all you'll be wanting today?' The groceries piled up on the counter between them, Eileen smiled warmly at the young woman who for once didn't seem in a particular hurry to rush away.

Holding out her money, Karen felt a faint flush stain her cheeks at being the recipient of such unstinting warmth. 'That's all, thank you. If I've forgotten anything I can always come back tomorrow, can't I?'

'Indeed you can. You'll be as welcome as the flowers in May, and that's the truth—though I can't help thinking it must be awful lonely, living up there in Paddy O'Connell's old cottage all on your own. You've been here for quite a while now, haven't you? What about your family? Sure, your poor mother must be missing you something awful.'

Smiling uneasily, Karen said nothing. Who was she to disenchant this lovely old lady of the idea that her mother must be missing her? The truth was that Elizabeth Morton was probably glad that her tragic daughter had moved to Ireland for the foreseeable future. That way, she wouldn't have to deal with all the messy, 'inconvenient' emotions she so clearly detested and that Karen's presence would inevitably bring up. With Karen settled in Ireland for a while, Elizabeth could fool herself that all was still well in the world. A world where she'd become a master at keeping up appearances and disguising her feelings—a realm where she could continue socialising and lunching with her friends as though tragedy had not hit her only child like a tidal wave and all but dragged her under.

Eileen Kennedy was too astute a woman not to see that the reference to her mother had unsettled Karen. Her reluctance in commenting easily conveyed that something had gone on there. Not that Karen blamed the shopkeeper for being curious. She'd often sensed that the locals she bumped into in the small but buzzing Irish town were curious about the 'aloof' English girl who had rented 'Paddy O'Connell's old place', as it was regularly referred to—not least of all the local lads who whistled and tried to engage her whenever she passed by. All Karen wanted was some peace and quiet, but people wouldn't know why unless she told them. And she wasn't ready to do that. Not by a long chalk.

'Now, love...' Carefully arranging the groceries in Karen's large wicker basket, Mrs Kennedy rang up the amount on the old-fashioned till—another charming relic from long ago. The cosy corner shop set-up was much more appealing to Karen than a soulless supermarket. As the elderly lady counted out her change, her watery blue eyes seemed to consider her un-smiling expression sympathetically. 'Please forgive me if you think I'm being too forward, but I get the distinct feeling that you could use some cheering up—and I have a suggestion. There's music and dancing down at Malloy's Bar just off the high street on Saturday night, and you'd be made as welcome as if you were one of our own. Why don't you come and join us? I'll be there about eight or so, with my husband, Jack, and we'd love you to come and sit with us. Sure, a bit of music and dancing would do you the world of good. Put the bloom back into those lovely cheeks of yours.'

Music... Inwardly, Karen sighed with longing. How she had missed it. But how could she return to it with any enjoyment after what had happened to Ryan? It had been eighteen months—eighteen long months since she'd even picked up her guitar. What if she couldn't sing again? What if the tragedy had robbed her of her voice for good? What was the point anyway? Karen's singing career had been her and Ryan's joint dream. Now that her husband was no longer living, she didn't have the heart to pursue it on her own. 'Tragic Princess of Pop' the local papers had dubbed her. Maybe that would always be the case. That was one of the reasons why she had eventually fled to Ireland—Ryan's homeland—selecting the most westerly and rural location she could find, where no one would have heard of the singer who had been starting to make a name for herself back home in Britain.

Now she sighed out loud, wishing with all her heart that she didn't feel so emotionally ambushed by a simple kind invitation to an evening out. If only she could be normal again—if only she could reply easily and with pleasure at the thought of being amongst people having a good time again. Her gaze focusing on the neat row of canned baked beans and tinned tomatoes behind Eileen Kennedy, she willed herself to say something. Anything. Before the kindly shopkeeper concluded she had lost her manners. But the lady behind the counter didn't seem in a hurry for a reply. All the shopkeepers Karen had met here had easily transmitted to her that there was nothing they liked better than passing the time of day with a customer.

Finally, sighing again deeply, she found the words she was searching for. 'I don't think so, Mrs Kennedy. It's very nice of you to ask me, but I'm—I'm not very good around people just now.'

'And sure, no one will expect anything different, sweetheart. They understand you've come here for your own private reasons. My guess is to get over something...or someone, maybe? No one expects you to be the life and soul of the party. If there's any nonsense from anyone my Jack will give them short shrift and no mistake! Come on, now—what could it hurt?'

That was the six-million-dollar question as far as Karen was concerned, and one she still hadn't figured out the answer to. What *was* certain was that she definitely wasn't ready to socialise yet—the way she was feeling she'd sooner jump out of a plane without a parachute. 'I can't. I appreciate you asking me, I really do, but right now I...I just couldn't.'

'Fair enough, dear. You come and join us when you're ready. We're always at Malloy's on a Saturday night, me and Jack, so we are.' Eileen rubbed her hands down her wraparound apron, its worn cotton fabric quaintly adorned with sprigs of red berries on a faded pink background, and smiled.

'Mrs Kennedy?'

'Yes, my dear?' The old lady leaned across the counter at the unexpected lowering of the younger woman's voice, resting her well-covered forearm on the scratched wooden surface.

Karen cleared her throat to give her courage. She respected everybody's right to privacy, she really did—she hated hers being invaded—but she suddenly had an imperative need to know about the man in the woods. The 'big bad wolf', as he'd sardonically dubbed himself.

'Is there a man in the area who owns a huge fawn-coloured dog? A Great Dane, he said it was.'

'Gray O'Connell,' Eileen replied without hesitation. 'His father lived in the very cottage you're staying in.'

'His father? You mean his father is Paddy O'Connell?' Karen frowned as a wave of shock shuddered through her.

'*Was*, you mean… Yes, Paddy was a fine man until the drink did for him—God rest his soul.' The old lady crossed herself, then leaned conspiratorially towards Karen. 'His son owns practically everything of any worth around here—including your cottage, of course. Not much pleasure it brings him, either. 'Tis a wonder he hasn't gone the way of his father himself, with all that's happened. But there, I expect he finds solace in his own way, with his painting and such.'

'He's an artist?'

'Yes, dear…a good one, too, by all accounts. My friend Bridie Hanrahan works up at the big house, cleaning and cooking for him. If it wasn't for Bridie we wouldn't hear anything about the man at all. Turning into a real recluse, he is. 'Tis true that money doesn't buy happiness. More than true in Gray O'Connell's case, I would say.'

Karen said nothing. It wasn't her business to pry, or to try and tease more information out of the effusive Mrs Kennedy. She'd heard enough to know that the man had good reason to keep himself to himself, and she of all people could respect that.

'Well, I'd better be going now. Thanks for everything, Mrs Kennedy.'

'Do you mind if I ask why you wanted to know about Gray O'Connell?'

Colouring hotly at the question, Karen let her glance settle momentarily on the fat barrel of rosy-red apples by the door, their overripe scent filling the shop.

'I take an early-morning walk in the woods sometimes. I bumped into him and his dog, that's all.' She wouldn't tell the other woman that she had been scared out of her wits at the sight of the pair of them.

'He's an early riser, too, so I hear.' Eileen shrugged one plump shoulder. 'I daresay he managed to keep a civil tongue in his head?'

'Just about.' Karen's expression was pained for a moment. 'I don't think he was feeling very sociable, either.'

'That sounds like your man. Don't pay any mind to his dark ways, will you? Once upon a time he was an entirely different kettle of fish, I can tell you, but tragedy has a way of knocking the stuffing out of folks, and that's the truth. Some are never the same again.'

I can vouch for that, Karen acquiesced silently. 'Well… thanks again, Mrs Kennedy. I'll be seeing you.'

'Take care of yourself, love. See you soon.'

And with the clanging of the bell behind her, Karen stepped out of the snug little shop, climbed into her car, and hurriedly headed home….

She didn't venture into the woods over the next few days. Instead she walked along the deserted beach, wrapped up warmly in sweater and jeans, waterproof jacket and gloves. It rained most mornings—a fine, drizzly affair that the locals lyrically referred to as a 'soft' rain—and the truth was Karen didn't let the weather bother her. It suited her sometimes melancholy frame of mind, and if she waited for the day to be fine she'd never get past the front door.

She'd taken to collecting shells here and there. Her gaze naturally gravitated to the delicate pretty ones, but lately she'd added a couple of bigger specimens to her collection. Taking them back to the cottage, she'd arranged them on the windowsills, and she swore the scent of the sea still clung to each one. But mostly she just walked along the fine white sand until her legs ached, with nothing but the infinitely wise music of the ocean and the gulls screeching above to keep her company.

Often, her thoughts turned to Ryan. Most days she thought sadly how much he would have loved sharing her morning walks. How he would have been keen to share his knowledge of local plants and wildlife with her and fuel her hungry imagination with tales of old Ireland, of kings and storytellers, of myths and magic. She learnt afresh that she'd lost her best friend as well as her husband and manager.

One morning on the beach she discovered she wasn't alone. Transfixed by the huge paw-prints dug deep into the sand, Karen felt her heart start to gallop. Shielding her eyes with her gloved hand against the diamond-bright glare of the sun, she glanced up ahead. There they were, just on the horizon, the 'big bad wolf' and his sidekick, Lurch. Karen grinned. She hadn't found much to laugh at during the past interminable few months, and it was strangely exhilarating feeling this sudden desire to dissolve into mirth.

Grinning again, she kicked at some seaweed, then strolled slowly across the wide expanse of sand to the edge of the beach. As the foamy sea lapped at her booted toes, she determinedly resisted the urge to glance up ahead again and see if the man and his beast had gone. Instead, she fixed her sights on the horizon, on the pair of little boats that bobbed up and down on the waves—fishermen, most likely. Men who regularly braved the vagaries of the sea to make their living. There was definitely something heroic about them, she decided. After idly watching them for a while, she silently wished them a good day's catch and turned to go.

She sucked in a surprised breath when she saw Chase pounding across the sand towards her. Behind him strode his master, and even with the distance between them Karen could see he was not best pleased. *Tough,* she thought, bracing herself for another terse encounter. But she was completely amazed and almost bowled over when Chase came to an abrupt halt just inches away from her. He sat back on his haunches with a look of such expectancy in his great dark eyes that Karen actually found herself smiling at the beast.

'You silly hound,' she murmured, reaching out to pat his head. To her relief, he didn't try and bite her hand off, but instead made a sort of contented gurgling sound in his throat almost like a cat purring. It made her laugh out loud.

'So...Little Red Riding Hood tames the beast.' Gray O'Connell stopped about a foot away from them to regard Karen with a half-amused, enigmatic glance.

Immediately wary, she stopped fussing over the huge dog and dug her hands deep into her waterproof. All of a sudden the urge to laugh at anything suddenly deserted her.

'Which beast are you referring to?' she asked boldly.

A dark eyebrow lifted mockingly. 'It would take more than a slip of a girl with pretty blue eyes to tame me, Miss Ford.'

'You know who I am, then?' Ignoring what she thought of as a distinctly backhanded compliment, Karen frowned.

'I should do. You're staying in my father's old cottage. I'm your landlord.'

If he'd thought to shock her, Karen had the advantage—

thanks to Eileen Kennedy. 'So I learned the other day, Mr O'Connell. And, by the way, I wish you'd stop referring to me as a girl. I'm twenty-six and very definitely a woman.'

She'd never meant for the latter part of her statement to sound petulant and annoyed, but somehow it did. All that was missing was the stamping of her foot. To her complete and utter embarrassment, Gray O'Connell threw back his dark head and laughed out loud. Whether that laugh had genuine humour in it was another matter. To Karen's mind, as she studied the handsome, sardonic profile, it sounded mockingly cruel.

'I'll take your word about you being a woman and not a girl, Miss Ford. Who can tell what's underneath that shapeless garment you're wearing?'

Karen's cheeks burned with indignation. 'There's no need to be so rude. It's just a waterproof. You'd hardly expect me to walk on the beach in this weather in something wispy and diaphanous, would you?'

The unsettling mercurial grey eyes insolently swept her figure. His jaw rose fractionally with undeniable challenge.

'It would take more than that to tame the beast in me, Miss Ford—but I feel myself warming to the idea by the second...'

'You're completely impossible!' This time, to her complete dismay, Karen did resort to stamping her foot. As soon as she'd done it she felt immensely foolish, and frustratingly too close to tears to say anything else. In front of her, Chase cocked his head, as if he understood and sympathised. It was funny how she was quickly warming to the dog and not the man.

'I'm afraid you're not the first woman to make that accusation,' Gray muttered darkly, 'and I'm damn sure you won't be the last. By the way, it's rather fortunate that we've seen each other today. There's something I wanted to tell you.'

'Oh?' Karen's brows knit worriedly beneath her honey-blonde fringe. 'And what would that be, Mr O'Connell?'

'I'm giving you notice to quit the cottage. Two weeks as of today. It's no longer available to rent.'

Thunder roared in her ears as she stared at Gray O'Connell's darkly implacable face in disbelief. He wanted her to leave the cottage? In just two weeks? Her plans had not been carved in stone, but she'd counted on staying where she was for at least another couple of months or so. To uproot now, when she was just starting to feel a part of this place... It was upsetting and unthinkable—and all because her devilish landlord had apparently taken an instant dislike to her!

'Why?' When the word came out she sounded winded, as if she'd been running. Disappointment and hurt tugged at the corners of her mouth, pulling it downwards.

Gray O'Connell shrugged one broad shoulder encased in battered black leather. 'As far as I'm aware I'm not legally bound to explain my reasons.'

'No, but it's common courtesy, surely?'

Those strange fey eyes of his glittered with chilling frostiness, openly scorning her indignation. 'Go back to your nice, safe little world in British suburbia, Miss Ford. Don't be fooled by the scenery or the supposed peace of this place. There is no peace to be had around here. Only heartache and tragedy and that's a fact. A place like this—a life like mine—has no time for such petty considerations as common courtesy!'

His words were released with such savagery that for a moment Karen didn't know what to do. There was one part of her that wanted to run away—to hasten back to the cottage and pack—yet there was also something perverse in her that willed her to stay and face him out, make him see that he wasn't the only one who was hurting. *Not that he'd listen to her, of course.* Not when he'd already clearly dismissed her as a silly little girl.

'Then I feel very sorry for you, Mr O'Connell.'

Her gaze lingered dangerously on the cold, unfeeling glance that was bereft of anything remotely akin to human warmth, then moved curiously down to the strongly patrician nose. It was a work of art, that was for sure... A fraction lower and her glance finally came to rest on the perfectly sculpted brooding mouth, whose upper lip was an uncompromising line of bitterness and hostility. With jolting awareness she saw that in spite of its currently bleak outlook he had a face that could be quite devastating in its beauty.

'I feel sorry for you...yes, sorry. It seems that you've forgotten what it is to be entirely human. My guess is that you're angry about something...hurt, too. But rage only creates more rage, you know. It hurts *you* more than it hurts anyone else. I don't know what's tormenting you, but I like your father's cottage... I'd really like to stay there for a little while longer. If it's more rent you want, then—'

'Keep your damn money, woman! Do you think I need it?'

He glanced bleakly out to sea for several long seconds, his jaw hard and angled with rage, his eyes glittering—a prisoner in his own morose, walled-off world. A man who had deliberately isolated himself from the rest of humanity and the comfort he might get from it. Karen was chilled right down to the bone. He was like an iceberg—remote, glacial and impervious. If she'd hoped to appeal to his better nature it was becoming glaringly obvious that he didn't have one.

That established, she started to turn away, surprised when Chase followed her for a few steps, whimpering as if he didn't want her to go.

'You've put a damn hex on my dog, you little witch.'

Gray's next words stopped her in her tracks. Karen sucked in an astonished breath.

'The sooner you go, the better, Miss Ford. Two weeks...
then I want you gone!'

He pivoted and strode off up the beach. The long legs that
were encased in fitted black denim jeans hinted at the powerful muscle in his thighs, and Chase, after one more sorrowful
glance at Karen, turned and raced after him...

CHAPTER TWO

THE day after Karen's second unfortunate encounter with Gray O'Connell, the cold that had been brewing for days arrived with a vengeance. Having had very little in the way of sleep the night before, she decided to be sensible for once and stay indoors. After a tiring struggle to get the ultimately feeble fire going, she flopped down wearily into the one worn, tapestry-covered armchair with its lacy antimacassar, nursing her mug of hot water and lemon, trying not to succumb to a strong wave of self-pity—a challenge when her eyes were droopy and red from lack of sleep and her nose was stinging and sore from blowing it.

Outside, the rain increased with sudden force, the branches of the trees creaking eerily beneath the weight of it. It was a desolate, lonely sound, but surprisingly it didn't bother her. Not when she was despondent because of something much more disturbing to her peace of mind. *She didn't relish the thought of leaving this old stone cottage.* It was so unfair when Gray O'Connell had only demanded she leave because he'd taken a personal dislike to her. What other reason could there be, when he hadn't even thought it necessary to explain?

Well, perhaps it would end up being for the best in the long run—his ill-mannered ways certainly didn't bode well for future encounters if she stayed. Even so, Karen would now have to search for another property to rent in the area.

Whatever happened, she wasn't ready to return home yet. Not when the inevitable questions and perhaps criticisms from family and friends would be waiting for her. She wasn't nearly ready to explain her feelings or her actions to anyone. The truth was she didn't know if she'd ever be ready for that. She'd struggled for over a year, pretending she was handling things, and in the end had realised she just had to get away.

Sometimes it had been hard to breathe, staying surrounded by the same old people and the same old scenery. She'd longed to escape.

Putting aside her drink, she sniffed gingerly into her handkerchief, doing her utmost not to irritate her already sore nose. The next instant the sniffing somehow manifested as a muffled sob, and before she knew it her heart was breaking once more. *She missed Ryan so much.* He'd been her constant companion, her rock. Her heart was submerged in a drowning wave she didn't have the strength to kick against. He'd been taken from her so suddenly and cruelly that they hadn't even had the chance to say goodbye. Her mind and body had been incarcerated in ice ever since. No one could comfort her. Not her mother, any of her family, or even well-meaning friends. *No one but Ryan.*

She held her arms across her middle, as if to comfort herself, but knew it was an ultimately useless exercise. Nothing could heal her heartache. Only the passing of time might blunt the edges of sorrow, and eventually when she was ready, the letting in of people who genuinely cared. The crumpled square of linen in her hands quickly became soggy with more tears.

When the knocker hammered in a staccato echo on the front door she froze in her seat, silently willing whoever it was calling on her in this foul weather to go away. The truth was, the way she was feeling, even stirring out of her seat required a colossal effort she didn't feel up to making right now.

When she didn't rise to see who it was the knocker hammered again. The sound cut like a scythe through Karen's already thumping head, making her wince. Hastily wiping her face with the damp, crumpled handkerchief, knowing miserably that she must look a wreck, she reluctantly roused herself to answer it.

Outside in the rain, droplets of water coursing down his coldly handsome face, his arms folded across his chest, Gray O'Connell leaned impatiently against the doorjamb. As Karen stared up at him in surprise, he straightened and jerked his head. 'Can I come in?'

Frankly amazed that he hadn't just barged in anyway, Karen nodded dumbly. Inside, the sitting room's crackling fire blazed a cosy welcome, despite the definite lack of sociability on the part of the house's tenant. Resignedly making her way back to the armchair, Karen resumed her seat. If only she wasn't feeling so pathetic she'd tell him to go away—even if he *did* own the house. She still had some rights as a tenant. Slowly Gray approached the fire. His jacket dripped onto the stone flagged floor. It was partially covered with a hand-woven rug that must have been beautiful and vibrant once, but was now a dull shadow of its former self.

Reluctantly Karen made herself speak. 'You'd better take off that jacket. You're soaked.' Heaving herself back onto her feet again, she forced herself to wait patiently as he reluctantly took it off. He handed it to her without a word, and she took it and hung it on the peg at the back of the door. It smelled of the wind, the rain and the sea, and for a wildly unsettling moment Karen fancied she could detect the arresting male scent of its owner, too. Surreptitiously she allowed her fingers to linger a little longer than necessary on the soft worn leather.

Turning back into the room, she was immediately struck by the intensely solitary picture that her visitor made. He was holding out his long-fingered hands to the fire and his handsome profile was marred by a look of such unremitting desolation that Karen's heart turned over in her chest. Why had he come here? she wondered. A feeling of desperation clutched her chest. What did he want from her? He'd already told her that he didn't want her as a tenant. There was no need to tell her again. She'd received the message loud and clear.

'I couldn't paint.' Turning briefly to regard her, almost instantly he returned his gaze to the fire, as though locked deep inside the prison of his own morose thoughts. 'Not today. And for once I didn't want to be alone.'

'I heard that you were an artist.'

'And I'm sure that's not *all* you heard. Am I right?' He shook his head disparagingly.

In spite of her innate caution, Karen moved hesitantly towards him, surprise and compassion making her brave. Suddenly the inexplicable need to offer this man comfort overshadowed everything—even her personal feelings of misery and pain.

'Is there anything I can do to help?'

'Help what? Free me from this incessant gloom that follows me everywhere? No. There's nothing you can do to help.'

His voice harsh, Gray pivoted away from the fire and started to pace the room. He was an imposing broad-shouldered man, with hair as black as tar—a dramatic hue that gleamed fiercely as though moonlight was on it—and his very stature made the already small room appear as though it had shrunk. The two of them might have been occupying a dolls' house.

'There's nothing you can do except maybe refrain from asking questions and be silent,' he uttered less irritably. 'I appreciate a woman who knows how to be silent.'

Intuitively Karen understood his need for quiet. She'd already registered the turmoil reflected painfully in his eyes and in the grim set of his mouth. This time she wasn't offended by his sharp words. On soft feet encased only in the thick white socks she wore beneath her jeans, she made her way back to the armchair and sat down. Gathering up the book that earlier on she'd been attempting to lose herself in, she laid it on the coffee table beside the chair and offered him a weak and watery smile.

'Okay…no questions, and I'll just sit here quietly.'

She might have meant it when she'd told him, that but it didn't stop Karen's mind from teeming with questions and speculations about her taciturn landlord. And heaven knew it was nigh on impossible to concentrate on anything else, with his brooding figure moving restlessly round, up and down in front of her.

'Why were you crying?'

The question pierced the silence that by mutual agreement had enveloped them. The sound of it reverberated through Karen like the shattering of glass.

'I wasn't crying,' she quickly denied, picking up her book again and staring unseeingly at the cover. 'I've got a cold.' She sniffed into her handkerchief as if to emphasise the point.

'You were crying,' Gray reiterated, his gaze steely. 'Don't you think I'm capable of knowing when a woman's been crying?'

'I don't know. I don't know anything about you.' She blinked sorrowfully down at the pale cold hands that covered the book in her lap and a shudder of distress rippled through her. Why did he have to call on her today of all days? It was said that misery loved company, but if only he would just go and leave her to her own misery in peace.

'I don't want you to know me, either.' He shook his head, as if warding off further unsettling thoughts, then glared at her.

Karen retreated even more inside herself. Wrenching her glance away, she stared back down at her book. She hadn't a hope in hell of reading any more of it today—at least not while her brooding landlord was taking up space in the house.

Gray exhaled deeply. 'You're probably thinking that's hardly fair, when I've invaded your own peace and quiet and you're clearly upset.'

'If you need to talk…just to have someone listen without judging or commenting…then I can do that,' she answered softly, her heart racing a little because she didn't know how he'd react.

'All right,' he said aloud, almost to himself. 'All right, then. I'll talk.' He breathed deeply, gathering his thoughts. 'My father lived in this house for five years before he died.' He stopped pacing to address her, his distant storm-tossed gaze restless and preoccupied. 'He'd never let me put things right. Liked it just as it was, he said…didn't want my money. He was mad at me because I didn't stay and work the farm that he used to own—until it got too much for him. The farm that his father and grandfather had owned before him. He didn't understand that those days were gone. Working the land wasn't in my blood like it was in his. I had other dreams. Dreams I wanted a chance at. Besides, a man can barely scratch a living out of farming these days—not when the supermarkets can undercut him at every turn and fly in cheap vegetables from Peru rather than buy them from local farms.'

His expression was scornful for a moment, and pressing his fingers hard into his forehead, he twisted his lips angrily. 'What had my fancy university education and my cleverness done for me? my father asked once. As far as he could see all it had accomplished was to send me away from this place— away from home.' He paused, as if weighing up the wisdom or indeed lack of it in proceeding with his story. In the end it seemed he'd decided to throw any caution he might be feeling to the wind. 'He wasn't interested that I'd made a fortune on the stockmarket. He asked me, "How much money does a man need to live a useful life?" I've been pondering that question ever since. I'm not sure how useful it is, but eventually I did find something to do with my life that gave me even more pleasure than making money. I discovered that I loved to paint, and lo and behold it turned out I had some skill at it! My desire to pursue it in the place I grew up finally brought me home, but it was too late for Paddy and me to be reconciled. He was too bitter and too full of regret at what he had lost, and the man was dead from drink three months after I returned. I found him dead down on the beach one morning, a half-bottle of whiskey in his pocket. He'd fallen against a rock and smashed his head.'

A lone tear splashed onto the cover of Karen's book. Gray's raw desolation merged with hers, welling up inside her like a dam strained to bursting. Missed opportunities, families torn apart, lost loves—it was all too much to bear.

'I'm sorry.'

'There's no need to be sorry for me. What I did…everything that happened…was down to my own selfish actions. Oh, hell!' Raking his fingers through the thick black mane that was still sodden from the rain, he shook his head. 'I don't know why I'm even telling you all this. I never did believe the adage that confession is good for the soul. Put it down to a momentary descent into madness and despair, if you like.'

'Sometimes it helps to talk.'

'Does it? I'm not so sure about that. But I can see how tempting it might be for a man to confide in *you*. That soft voice and quiet way you seem to possess suggests you might be capable of easing pain…for a while at least. Not that *I'm* looking for that.' He regarded her suspiciously for a moment, his voice scathing.

'Believe me…I'm no expert at healing anybody's pain, and I wouldn't pretend that I was.' Stung, Karen dipped her head.

'Then we're even, aren't we? Because I'm not looking to be healed. So don't make the mistake of thinking that's what I came for.' Throwing her a brief warning glance, Gray O'Connell stalked to the door and grabbed his still wet jacket almost violently off the peg.

Ignoring the insult, Karen immediately got to her feet, her book tumbling unheeded to the floor. 'Perhaps—perhaps you'd like to stay and have a cup of tea with me?' she offered uncertainly, her smile unknowingly engaging.

The stark expression of raw need in those startling grey eyes impaled her to the floor. A red lick of heat kindled and grew inside her—heat that transcended her cold and the feeble state her body was currently in and put twin flags of searing scarlet into her cheeks.

'Tea's not what I need, Miss Ford. And something tells me you're not the kind of woman who'd be willing to offer me exactly what it is I do need right now...'

He didn't need to explain. The force of his desire was as palpable as a storm about to break.

He pulled on his dripping jacket, then yanked open the door with unnecessary force. 'And, by the way, you can stay here as long as you like. Stay or go—it's up to you. I don't really care one way or the other.'

Catching the edge of the door, Karen unhappily watched him go, head down, striding off into the rain, like a man whose broad shoulders were weighted down with the cares of the world. Shockingly, she wished she knew a way to make him stay. The thought made her heart thump hard inside her chest. *If her landlord had descended into temporary madness then apparently so had she.* It was jolting to realise that craving bold glance he'd shot her just now had had the power to make her feel aroused. Or was it just that it had been so long since a man had regarded her with desire in his eyes?

After Ryan had died she'd told herself she'd never want or need a man again. And it was hard to believe Gray O'Connell of all men wanted *her*...especially in her current unappealing state. Her usually glossy fair hair had lost its lustre, whilst her cold made her resemble some half-starved waif who needed to be tucked up in bed with a hot water bottle and a steaming bowl of broth—never mind a man with winter-grey eyes and a look fierce enough to quell even the indomitable Queen Boudicca.

Her body grew warm at his assessment that she wasn't the kind of woman who could offer him exactly what he'd needed right then. *How did he know that she couldn't?* Spending night after night cold and lonely and hurting in her bed was apt to make a grieving woman slightly crazy.

Karen sucked in a startled breath as she realised she could even contemplate such a thing with a man who was practically a stranger—especially when only minutes before she'd been breaking her heart over Ryan. Reluctantly closing the door, she leant back against the wooden panelling and shut her eyes. Any port in a storm—that was all Gray O'Connell was looking for. And maybe at the end of the day so was she. The man she'd loved and married was long gone. Maybe any port in a storm was all she could hope for now?

But at least her brooding landlord had said she could stay— even if he *had* thrown his decision at her like a scrap of meat from his plate. There was really no need for her to feel so stupidly grateful but the fact remained that she was...she *was*.

On Saturday, Karen made a more prolonged visit to the thriving local town. Elated by her landlord's grudging permission to let her stay on at the cottage, she vowed she'd celebrate by buying some new bits and pieces to cheer the place up. When she left she'd leave them for whoever came after her, but while she was there they would help make the house feel more like home.

With that thought in mind, she browsed contentedly around the quaint narrow streets and thoroughfares, dipping in and out of enticing little craft shops and bookshops, sampling textures, scents and colours, sometimes buying—sometimes not.

Much of the time her exploration was accompanied by the uplifting Irish tunes that drifted out from many of the pubs she passed. The music stirred her soul, as it had always done. It made her happy and sad simultaneously. Happy for the fierce joy it brought her, and sad because she'd probably left that way of life behind for good. But still the fingers that curled round the strap of her shoulder bag itched to pick up a guitar and play, and she had a brief vision of the instrument tucked away beneath her bed.

Squashing the thought, Karen drifted into a coffee shop for a latte and a Danish pastry, content to sit amongst strangers with lilting Irish voices and enjoy her refreshment in peace.

When she came out again the light was slowly fading, and people were starting to head home. On a last-minute impulse she dived into the bookshop she'd spied on the way across the street to the coffee shop and purchased a little book that had given her some much needed consolation in the months directly after Ryan's death. Unfortunately she'd left her copy back in the UK. Tucking the book carefully into her bag, she made her way tiredly but contentedly back to where she'd parked the car.

Lifting the lid on the simmering pot of stew, with its delicious and mouthwatering aroma of braised lamb and fragrant herbs, Karen took a deeply appreciative sniff, hearing her stomach growl in response. Her day out had given her the appetite of a Titan, and she was so glad that she'd thought to make dinner the night before, because now all she had to do was let it properly heat through and enjoy it.

In the tiny sitting room scented candles flickered on almost every surface, the mingled scents of sandalwood, musk and vanilla creating a soothing ambience of warmth and relaxation, which was exactly what Karen had hoped for. Now that she'd got over her cold she was fully committed to taking much better care of herself—not just eating sensibly and taking regular exercise, but learning how to relax properly. Something she had never really done up until now.

Her life with Ryan had been wonderful, but the last couple of years before he'd died it had been pretty much commitment after commitment, with barely a blank space in the diary to call their own. Touring up and down the country had taken its toll, and Karen had for ever been promising herself that one day she would definitely make more time for herself. Well, now she had the opportunity.

The atmosphere in the cottage was strangely evocative. It brought to mind images of past times—of an older, more simple way of life, when people had worked the land and, even though they'd struggled to make ends meet, there had been a real sense of community and pulling together to help each other. A sense of sadness lingered in the rooms, too—a melancholy air that was like the wisp of smoke after a candle had been blown out. Karen yearned to do everything in her power to dispel that sadness if she could.

The story of Gray O'Connell's father Paddy had been on her mind ever since he'd related it, and she had an ache in her heart that hadn't left since she'd heard it. It was all too easy to imagine the man living here alone, with nothing but his memories and his whiskey to keep him company. No doubt Paddy had sorely missed his son when he'd left to make his fortune. In his case, accomplishing exactly that. In all probability the older O'Connell had been proud of his son's achievements, but maybe he just hadn't had the words or the courage to tell him? It was a shame that Gray was torturing himself over what had happened.

At the end of the day everyone had a choice in how they

responded to life's challenges, Karen reflected, and if his father had sought solace in whiskey then that had been his decision and was nothing to do with his son. That said, Gray O'Connell was clearly a troubled man himself.

He was so different in every way from her gentle loving Ryan. She tenderly recalled how her husband had had a real talent for communicating with people, and had always been able to find an encouraging word for anyone downhearted or in despair. In the music business, a temperament like his had been rare. She was so lucky to have had him in her life, if only for all too brief a time.

Exhaling a long, slow breath, she was gratified to see that her efforts at building the fire that evening were impressive, to say the least. Right now the flames were licking high and fierce into a really good blaze, rendering the room snugly warm as a result. In the background Karen's portable radio added muted sounds of conversation and laughter, and for the first time in a long time she was genuinely at ease. By that she meant she wasn't yearning for anything—not even company.

Her gaze roamed the room with satisfaction. The three small prints she'd purchased, of three different but equally beautiful traditional stone cottages, all set in the emerald-green landscape of the country, had been carefully arranged side by side above the fireplace. Sitting gracefully in a simple but elegant glass vase she'd found in a junk shop were a mixed bunch of cream and red roses, their evocative, fragrant scent mingling gently with the aromatic candles. They were just small, perhaps insignificant things in themselves, but the pleasure they gave Karen was immense.

Combing her fingers through her newly washed honey-gold hair, she glanced ruefully down at the faded blue jeans and red sweater she was wearing. Both items had definitely lost a little of their shape after several washes. The clothing had taken on the comfortable qualities of a dear old friend. Not that she had many 'dear old friends' to call upon since Ryan had gone. She grimaced. It was strange how bereavement either brought people closer or pushed them away.

Shaking off the thought, she wondered if she shouldn't make more than a passing concession to her new mood of optimism and change into something a little more feminine. There were two very nice Indian cotton dresses in her wardrobe—one dark green with a red velvet inlay on the bodice, and the other a rich luxurious purple that she'd bought in Camden Market back home. It might be nice to wear one of them to highlight all the good things she'd done for herself that day.

Contemplating a quick visit to the bedroom to change, she nearly jumped out of her skin when someone rapped on the door. Lifting the latch, she was greeted by the night, the bitter cold air and a handsome if austere Gray O'Connell.

'I came by to tell you that I've bought some things for the cottage. Is it okay if I drop them round in the morning?'

He addressed her without preamble, not even saying hello. Karen stared, feeling an answering jolt in her stomach when her glance collided with his. She'd never seen such heartfelt loneliness in a person's eyes. It didn't help that she knew some of the reasons for that achingly distant look.

'Sure—of course. Tomorrow morning's fine.' What he'd bought and why she couldn't guess, but somehow that seemed irrelevant right now.

'Good.' He turned away, not even bothering with goodbye, and for reasons she couldn't begin to analyse Karen found herself reluctant to let him go.

'I've made some stew for supper.' She faltered over the words as hectic colour suffused her face, fully aware that she had his attention more completely than a hunter fixing his sights on his prey before aiming his gun. Inwardly, she gulped. 'There's more than enough for two—that is if you haven't already eaten?'

'Is this a habit of yours?'

'What?'

'I mean do you normally extend spontaneous invitations to people you hardly know?' Gray demanded irritably, booted feet firmly set on her doorstep like a captain at the helm of his ship.

'You showed up the other day and came in without me inviting you. Is that any different?'

'I asked you if I could come in and you said yes.'

'Of course I did...you're my landlord. So I do know you, don't I?'

'Damn it, woman, you're on your own out here!'

He spoke as though she was far too relaxed about her personal safety for his liking. Karen was taken aback by the vehemence in his tone. Anyone who didn't know them would think that he *cared* whether she was safe or not—which was utterly ridiculous when one considered the facts.

'I know I'm perfectly safe here.' She kept her voice deliberately soft. 'I've only felt anxious once, and that was when I inadvertently crossed paths with the "big bad wolf" in the woods one day.'

For a moment a muscle tensed, then relaxed again in the side of Gray's high sculpted cheekbone. One corner of his mouth quirked upwards in the beginnings of a smile. The gesture made him sinfully, dangerously attractive, and Karen had cause to question her wisdom at so recklessly inviting him to join her. Just then she remembered an adage she'd once read that the most dangerous wolves were the ones who were hairy on the inside. Maybe she'd be wise to remember that?

'And he let you go?' Gray parried dangerously.

Karen caught her breath. 'Yes...he let me go.'

'One day those big blue eyes are going to get you into a barrel full of trouble, little girl.'

'I'm not a little girl, so stop calling me one. I'm a woman… a woman who's been married, for goodness' sake!'

'Have you? Are you telling me you're divorced now, then?' With an impenetrable glint in his eye he shouldered past her into the sitting room.

Mentally counting to five, Karen slowly closed the door on the cold, rainy night outside. She shivered hard, but it was nothing to do with the weather. Glancing across at her visitor, she saw that he'd taken off his jacket and thrown it casually across the threadbare arm of the couch. Once again he moved across to the fire and held out his hands to its warmth—though Karen privately thought it would take a lot more than even a hundred blazing fires to warm the icy river that must pass for blood in Gray O'Connell's veins.

'I'm a widow.' Finally commanding his full attention, she lightly shrugged a shoulder as he turned to survey her.

'How long since you lost your man?' It sounded almost poetic, the way he phrased it.

'Eighteen—nearly nineteen months ago.' She unfolded her arms to thread her fingers nervously through her hair, mentally bracing herself to receive some sort of barbed reply from this enigmatic man who clearly had so many defences that it was a wonder anything could pierce even a chink of his heavy armour. Not that she was looking for sympathy or anything.

'Is that why you came here?' His eyes raked her figure from head to foot, then returned to her face, where they reflected a provocatively unsettling interest in her mouth.

Karen grimaced uncomfortably. 'Now, about that stew…I hope you're hungry—'

'How did he die?' Though he stood-stock still, Gray's relentless gaze ate up the distance between them as though channelling electricity—probing her reluctance to give him the information he sought with all the steely-eyed determination of a professional interrogator.

'I don't—I don't really want to talk about it.' She dipped her head, twisting her fingers into a long burnished strand of hair, then impatiently pushing it away again. Her troubled gaze studied the once colourful swirls woven into the homespun rug at her feet with exaggerated concentration.

'I seem to remember you advising me that it sometimes helps to talk?'

Glancing up at him, Karen was inexplicably annoyed that he should throw what had, after all, been genuine compassion and concern back in her face.

'You didn't buy that idea when I offered it to you—why should you expect me to be any different in return?'

'In my own case I knew it wouldn't be of any use. You, however, are an entirely different case, Miss Ford. By the way, what *is* your first name?'

'You obviously know that it's Karen. You're my landlord. The letting agents must have informed you.'

'Perhaps I wanted to hear it from your own lips.' Curling his fingers round the thick black leather belt he wore round his jeans, Gray seriously considered her. 'You barely look old enough to have been married—let alone widowed.'

'You know how old I am. I've already told you. And Ryan and I were married for five years. His death came as a terrible shock. There was no warning, so I wasn't prepared. He hadn't even been ill. He worked hard…too hard. Long hours, with not enough rest—but that's the culture nowadays, isn't it?'

Her eyes glazed over with distress. 'The culture we're all taught to so admire. As if there's such virtue in working hard and dying young! My husband suffered a massive heart attack at the age of thirty-five. Can you imagine that? When he went, I wanted to die, too. So don't stand there and tell me I don't look old enough to be married, because in the space of those five short years with my husband I lived more life than most people do in ten times as long!'

She was shaking, emotion slamming into her like a train, appalled at giving in to such a passionate display in front of a man who probably regarded such outbursts as a certain sign of weakness…or at least a serious character flaw. If only she could take the words back, keep them private and unsaid, but it was clearly too late for that.

His handsome visage a cool, impenetrable mask of enforced self-control, Gray retrieved his jacket from the couch and wordlessly shrugged it on. As Karen struggled to regain even a shred of her former equilibrium, he came towards her, his expression grim. With her heart in her mouth she automatically stepped back. She saw the glimmer of disquiet in his gaze when she did, as if it took him aback that she might be afraid of him.

'I'm sorry for your trouble, Miss Ford, and sorry that I clearly intruded where I had no right. I didn't come here to make you revisit painful memories and upset you. I'll see you in the morning as arranged—if that's still all right? If not, we can leave it for another time that's more convenient.'

Nodding miserably, Karen plucked the material of her soft wool sweater between trembling fingers, twisting it into a knot. 'Tomorrow morning will be fine.'

'Good. I'll wish you goodnight, then.' Gray's glance greedily swept her pale solemn face, the distressed China-blue eyes with their long dark blonde lashes that reminded him of a fawn, and the full, almost pouting, trembling lips devoid of so much as a trace of lipstick. *A man would have to go a long way to find such innocent unaffected beauty in a woman*, he thought.

Karen heard him go to the door, lift the latch and step outside. As he went, her body seemed suddenly to move of its own volition, and she found herself hurrying after him. Out into the rainy night she ran, her eyes squinting up at the water that splashed onto her face, ignoring the cold, ignoring the wind that tore into her hair, sweeping the long sun-kissed strands into a dishevelled cloud.

'Gray!'

The voice that called out his name was full of anguish and something else—something that Gray registered in his mind with tight-lipped control. Heat seared him like a brand at the realisation, making him rock-hard with need. He turned to survey her. Even in the dark he knew his light-coloured eyes burned as brazenly as a cat's.

'What is it?'

'I just—I just want you to—'

'Don't ask me to stay, Karen. I'll only end up hurting you. Trust me.'

Her lip wobbled as she struggled for the words to tell him what she felt. 'I want— I need— Dear God! Do I have to spell it out for you?'

She was crying even as she spoke, her tears mingling with the rain. Why was it so hard to just say what she wanted? She missed the physical side of married life. She missed having someone to hold her and touch her and make her feel like a woman again. She didn't want a relationship with Gray O'Connell. He was the last man on earth she could ever want that with. He was too angry—too wounded to be kind. But they'd both been hurt by life. Why shouldn't they find comfort in each other's arms for a little while? It didn't have to mean any more than that, did it?

'It would only be sex, sweetheart,' Gray asserted coldly, as if intuiting her thoughts. 'Nothing else. Not "making love", not hearts and flowers and violins... Just sex. *Screwing*, plain and simple. Would you really settle for that?'

Shock slammed into Karen at his words. The strength

seemed to drain out of her legs completely. Yet she stood her ground, blinking back tears, blinking back the rain that had already left a fine damp sheen on her sweater, soaking its way onto her skin.

'Were you always this cruel?' she asked boldly into the night. 'I'll bet you pulled the wings off dragonflies when you were a boy. I'll bet you laid traps for poor defenceless animals... I bet you broke your poor mother's heart!'

In two strides Gray was in front of her, his dark face just inches away from hers, his warm breath fanning her face, making little clouds of steam in the rain. 'My mother took her own life when I was three. Maybe having me was to blame? Who knows? But whether it was me or my father I'll never know, and I have to live with that every day. So my advice to you, Karen, would be to think twice before you make such a throwaway comment again, damn you!'

The impact of the bitter words made Karen go rigid. Then, hardly realising what she was doing, she slowly raised her hand tentatively to touch his lips with her fingertips. They were infinitely soft to the touch—soft, but inherently stubborn. *Velvet clad in iron.* But right then she saw past the anger of the man, past the torment of the grown-up who didn't know where to go with his pain, and instead saw the small three-year-old boy who had been abandoned by his mother and ultimately abandoned by his father, too. Grief twisted her heart.

Gray grabbed her wrist to wrench her hand roughly away. Before she could react he wove his hands through the damp tresses of her hair to crush her lips beneath his mouth in a bruising, destroying kiss that made her body go limp with dazed reaction and turned her blood into a river of seething, molten desire so hot she thought she would be consumed by the sheer, staggering ferocity of it.

His tongue mercilessly swept the soft warm recesses of her mouth, taking brutal hostage of her flesh and her senses with all the insatiable relentless hunger of a man who'd gone without meat or drink for days—tearing into her with passion, demanding everything, sparing her nothing, until her heart pounded in her chest as if she was riding in a speeding car bent on crashing. When his hands left her hair and moved downwards to drag her hips hard against his, his manhood surged like steel against the giving flatness of her belly, leaving Karen in no doubt of the heat and the hardness in him. A kind of drugging sensuality rolled over her like a wave, robbing her of the power to think, to rationalise, to remain sane.

'Was it like this with your husband, Karen?' As he tore his mouth from hers Gray's eyes burned down at her as though in the grip of a fever. He ignored the rain that was soaking them both as though it didn't even exist. His midnight lashes blinked the moisture away temporarily.

It took several moments for Karen even to register the question. Her lips were aching and bruisingly tender from his passion, her body crushed against his hard, lean length as his arms held her captive, and it was hard to even remember who she was… *Tragic Karen Ford from suburban England—a woman who wrote lyrics about passion, who sang songs all about the kind of love that consumed body and soul but had never personally experienced herself.*

The shocking realisation was both a revelation and a trauma. It was as though she was utterly betraying Ryan's memory by even contemplating it. A sudden vision of her husband's tender smile imposed itself on her mind, cutting through the sensual fog that enveloped her. It made her twist urgently out of Gray's embrace to call a halt to the madness. Disgusted with herself for almost succumbing to nothing more than base lust, Karen wiped the back of her hand across her still throbbing lips.

Moving several steps away from the man who had only

moments ago taken her body hostage, she anxiously straightened her sweater, pushed back her hair to tidy herself, and tried desperately to summon back the woman who always strove to do the right thing, who didn't give way to wild, uncharacteristic impulses that threatened to land her in a cauldron of hot water that would scar her for ever and play havoc with her soul.

'My husband was a good, kind man.'

'But it's plainly not kindness you want from me, Karen—is it?'

Gray's lips twisted mockingly, and Karen felt a shaft of pain pierce her heart like a hot red spike.

'Don't.'

'Don't what?' he demanded derisively, hands either side of his hips, an imposing dark figure dressed in black, his sombre face a pale, startling contrast in the eerily atmospheric light of the moon. 'You've got to decide, Karen. Either you're just a girl or you *are* a woman. When you know the answer perhaps we can come to some mutually satisfying arrangement?'

'I don't want—I mean I'm not interested in—'

'Liar.' He spat the word out like a poisoned dart headed straight for her heart, making Karen feel deeply, unforgivably ashamed of her own wanton nature. A nature she'd had no trouble keeping under strict control when she was married to gentle, undemanding Ryan, with his beguiling smile and soft voice. Yet in a few short minutes with this hard unyielding stranger that unknown trait had burst free like some wild wind, sweeping everything aside in its path—including her dignity and common sense...

'I think you should leave.' Her words made a liar of her, too, because even now her body was craving Gray's touch as powerfully as any drug a person could be addicted to in spite of her shame and remorse.

'Yes, I think perhaps I should.'

With a distant look in his eyes that told her he wasn't even seeing her any more, Gray pivoted abruptly and disappeared into the rainy night as if he had been nothing but a disturbing figment of Karen's fevered imagination, conjured up by her longing and her loneliness.

Biting back a sob as she turned unhappily back towards the house, she knew with certainty that in her rational everyday mind there was no way on this good green earth that she would ever have conjured up a man like Gray O'Connell. Only a fool could expect anything more than hurt from such an angry, embittered soul as him....

CHAPTER THREE

GRAY splashed whiskey into a tumbler about a quarter of the way up the glass, then raised it to his lips. Despising himself for succumbing to a device that really was a last resort in his book, he took one long draught, emptied the glass and set it carelessly back down on the old oak sideboard. An answering fire burned in his gut, but even that wasn't hot enough to scorch out what ailed him. Just what did he think he'd been doing, treating a grieving young widow as if she was his for the taking? Just because she'd done him the courtesy of listening to his litany of regrets when he'd turned up unannounced at the cottage that first time, it didn't mean that he should presume she would now give him anything he asked for!

He groaned out loud, shaking his head. Chase looked up curiously from his place by the fire, then dropped his head mournfully down onto his front paws again as if to say *What's the point?*

Precisely… What *was* the point? Gray agonised. There were plenty of likely women in the town and thereabouts—women who would be only too willing to warm his bed. Some of them had done just that—if only briefly—in the past. After Maura had left him he hadn't cared about who they were, just that they were willing.

He almost reached for the whiskey bottle again at the thought of such recklessness. He'd protected himself, of course—he didn't want anyone jumping up and down accusing him of making them pregnant—but just the same it wasn't the kind of behaviour he was proud of.

But now, after two years of being unattached and heart-free—he scowled at that—he couldn't believe he could be so affected by a little witch with honey-gold hair and an angelic smile, and a body that he ached to have wrapped round him naked. Neither the faded jeans nor the baggy shapeless sweater she'd been wearing had been able to totally disguise the long-legged, shapely body beneath the clothes. It had taken every ounce of willpower Gray had in him to refrain from taking her out there in the rain—up against the wall of the cottage, most likely. Desire had been running high in both of them, like sizzling sparks along a fuse wire. He'd felt it in every exquisite tremble of that taut and sexy little body of hers. Gray imagined her big blue eyes widening in shock, then capitulating in passion as she opened to receive him.

The vivid picture he conjured up had heat slamming into him with such ferocity that there wasn't a single cell in his body that didn't want her right there and then—that wouldn't have pushed aside every single scruple he had left just to lose himself in the heat and softness of that alluring young body even as her sweetly musky scent drove him slowly crazy.

He was a passionate man—a man who put his heart and soul into everything he did, whether it was pushing his body hard in a workout, making money, painting pictures or making love. But he could honestly not recall another time in the whole of his thirty-six years when he had wanted a woman as badly as he wanted the chaste little widow. And the damnedest thing about it was that he had no business wanting her at all. Not when she was clearly still nursing her hurt over the death of her husband. Only a heartless bastard would take advantage of such a situation, and that was one title he'd tagged himself with for long enough.

'She's nothing but trouble with a capital T,' he said out loud, his rich, resonant tone ringing out in the big, sombre drawing room with its dark oak panelling and ruby-red carpeting. For such an impressive room, its furnishings were sparse, to say the least. A more kindly observer might suggest minimalist. One large antique couch sat a few feet back from the huge brick fireplace with its open hearth, its once deep red cushions now sadly flattened and faded to a more sedate and dusky plum.

There was nothing comfortable about it, if the truth be known, but then Gray had become so careless of his own comfort of late that he scarcely gave the matter much thought. A few once beautiful but now faded Turkish rugs were laid indifferently here and there across the rich carpet, and one large oak sideboard and a heavily embossed armchair—renovated for Maura's benefit, not *his*—was the only other furniture. On the walls were various old portraits that he'd got as a kind of 'job lot' when he'd purchased the grand old house, but none of them was of any relation of his as far as he knew. He'd been meaning to put them into storage, but lately he hadn't had the heart to even *think* about the task, let alone do it.

The house was beautiful, right enough. It had the kind of faded grandeur that many old Irish houses descended from the landed gentry often possessed. But now many of the owners of such houses couldn't afford the soaring upkeep they entailed, and despite the fact that Gray could afford it easily it was still soulless when all was said and done—even with his housekeeper Bridie's loving administrations. What else could it be with just one singularly unhappy man and his bear of a dog living in it? It occurred to him just then that his father's cottage was far more homely and welcoming. But then that was down to his beautiful shapely tenant and nothing to do with him.

As a picture of Karen filled his mind, scented candles and

blazing fire an alluring backdrop, he shook his head with a fresh spurt of anger, desperately trying to dismiss it. He couldn't understand it. The woman set him on fire with just one innocent glance from those incandescent blue eyes of hers. Doubly so because there was no falsity to be detected anywhere in their crystal silky depths—just a warmth he wanted to gravitate towards and a hurt that he found himself desperate to ease. That wasn't like him. *It wasn't like him at all.*

Besides, it was as plain as day that she didn't need a hard, embittered man like Gray. The woman's trusting soul and generous heart needed a man more in the mould of the way he guessed her husband must have been. Someone gentle and loving, no doubt—someone with infinite patience, someone selfless who worshipped the ground her perfect little feet walked on.

A rueful grin split his lips. The thick white socks she'd been wearing on a previous occasion hadn't gone unnoticed. She had feet like a ballerina, perfectly poised, with a delicate but distinct little arch that was positively sexy. He wondered what she'd look like wearing nothing else but those chaste white socks and that beguilingly angelic little smile of hers? The thought caused him serious agony. *For God's sake! Just give her a wide berth from now on, man!*

The instruction careened through his brain, wiping the grin clean off his handsome face. Scowling, Gray turned and stalked across the sea of ruby-red carpet, heading determinedly for the large scullery-type kitchen to chop up some steak for Chase's dinner....

Karen sat in the window seat sipping her tea, straining for the sound of the ocean, which on a calm, still day could just be detected by those of a soulful enough disposition wanting to hear it. Her whole body was tense with waiting. Waiting for Gray O'Connell to show up with whatever bits and pieces of furniture he wanted to install in the cottage. Perhaps after last night he'd changed his mind?

Her heart took a dive as she remembered how vulnerable she'd made herself to the man, how incapable she'd been of holding back the tide of feeling so strong that it had threatened to knock her off her feet. *Was that what passion did to a person?* Made them lose their reason and dignity?

If Gray hadn't strode away when he had, like some compelling black shadow melting into the darkness, Karen had serious doubts as to whether she would have restrained herself from practically *begging* him to share her bed. No wonder she was so keyed-up at the idea of seeing him again. How on earth was she even going to be able to look him in the eye? As if the man didn't have enough advantages, without his sexually frustrated tenant throwing herself at his feet!

With a little groan she shook her head, then scrubbed at the condensation from her breath that clouded the windowpane. Everything could do with a coat of paint, she thought suddenly, her glance assessing. The white emulsion on the small square frames was grey and flaking, and the same washed-out tone on the walls was equally ready for some kind of springlike makeover. Would it be presumptuous of her to ask her taciturn landlord if she could apply a fresh coat of paint here and there? she wondered. After all, it could only be to his advantage. She was quite prepared to buy the paint and undertake the task herself.

The sound of a vehicle approaching had her leaping off the seat and hurrying to the kitchen sink to empty her half-consumed mug of tea. Pulling out a drawer, she let her fingers busily scramble through the jumbled contents that consisted of matchbooks, packets of incense and the odd battery and paperclip, to reach for her hairbrush. She pulled the cushioned comb through her hair, wincing at the occasional tangle it wouldn't easily unravel.

Squinting into the small make-up mirror she'd left propped up against a line of cookery books on a shelf above the fridge, she grimaced at her flushed cheeks and over-bright eyes. It was hardly the composed visage she so desperately needed to present to her intimidating landlord, with his rangy good-looks and stinging glance that was currently the major stumbling block and disruption to her peace of mind.

A loud rapping on the door had Karen dropping the hair-brush haphazardly back into the drawer and slamming it shut with a bit too much gusto, causing the ill-fitting container to get jammed halfway and then refuse to budge. Cursing her own impatience, she left it as it was, then flew out into the sitting room to get the door.

'Hello!' Breathless, she stared up at Gray, winded by her sudden exertion as well as an unsettling feeling of intense anticipation at seeing him again.

Those mysterious grey eyes of his considered her for several tension-filled seconds without him uttering a word. *Was he even going to say hello back?* Karen's stomach lurched, then lurched again. Dry-mouthed, she let her gaze move down-wards to the deliberately provocative curl of those ruthless brooding lips. The same mocking lips that only just last night had all but burned her, highlighting an aspect of her nature that she now knew without a doubt she'd long suppressed.

'My, my… What big eyes you have, Miss Ford.' His voice, low and laced with a deliberate taunt, turned the blood in her veins to the consistency of sluggish warm treacle.

'Barring the name—isn't that supposed to be my line?' she quipped back, astounded that she'd managed to even get the words past her throat. Trouble was, she was remember-ing the provocative, compelling taste of that taunting mouth and wondering how she was going to pretend that nothing disturbing had happened when they both knew it had. That destroying, passionate kiss from Gray had turned everything

Karen believed about herself on its head, and there didn't seem to be a single thing she could do to restore that belief to where it had been before.

After assessing her for a couple more seconds, Gray bestowed upon her a disturbing lingering smile. 'A man could quite forget his own name, standing here looking at you,' he ruefully told her. 'And that wouldn't do. It wouldn't do at all. Regarding the furniture that I've brought—if you don't like it, or it's not to your taste, then I'll change it for something that suits better. Not that I'm enamoured of the idea of a shopping trip any time soon, but maybe for you, Miss Ford, I'll make an exception.'

'I'm sure whatever style you've chosen will be just fine,' she murmured, the mere *idea* of going on a shopping trip with Gray O'Connell churning her insides like butter.

'Good.' He grinned. 'What a refreshing change to meet a woman that's so amenable.' Turning abruptly, he stepped back outside.

When she finally remembered to breathe again, Karen's breath was distinctly shaky. There was no doubt that the man was good-looking—if in a kind of arrogant, couldn't-care-less, everybody-else-be-damned kind of way—but when he smiled... His smile was like the sun lighting up the greyest of gloomy days, or a full moon brightly showcasing the myriad stars that it shared the night sky with. His fathomless long-lashed eyes were stop-you-in-your-tracks amazing, and his mouth—his mouth had a deliciously enigmatic curve that was without a doubt provoking and made her toes curl. It also transformed his face from darkly handsome to hauntingly, irresistibly beautiful. *How could a woman ever forget it?* All Karen could do was blink up at him, saying nothing. It was as if she had suddenly lost the power to *think*, let alone speak, when he looked at her like that.

Striding across the grassy area round the house onto the

narrow unmade road that led to the dwelling, Gray opened the rear doors of a large white transit van. Karen saw a tall, slim young man with a thatch of unruly fair hair, dressed in paint-splattered jeans and a scruffy black tee shirt, clamber out of the front seat and amble up beside him—presumably to assist with whatever he'd brought in the van.

The first item to emerge was a beautiful Victorian two-seater sofa with cabriole legs, upholstered in natural linen. Its condition was immaculate, and between the two of them the men brought it into the house and deposited it beside the older worn version that it would replace. Lifting the three small green velvet cushions that adorned the old couch, Gray threw them down onto its smarter replacement, then glanced directly over at Karen where she stood awkwardly and bemused by the door.

'That's a lot better, don't you think?'

There was something almost endearing about the glance Gray gave her—almost as if he was unsure of her reaction and sought her approval. The thought was so surprising that an answering sensation of warmth curled in Karen's belly, bringing with it a surge of affection towards the aloof, complex man who acted as if he didn't need anything from anyone—let alone affection.

'It's great.' She lifted her shoulders with a shrug of pleasure.

'By the way, this is Sean Regan. Sean—meet Miss Ford.'

'Call me Karen.' She stepped forward to shake the younger man's hand, already warming to the unrestrained friendliness she saw on his eager, attractive face, and noting the two little silver earrings he wore in one earlobe with a feeling almost akin to maternal indulgence. Which was ridiculous, because he could only be a couple of years her junior—if that.

Her shy gaze slid furtively across to Gray. Perhaps it was just that she preferred her men to be a little more mature and rugged? Gray certainly fitted into that criteria as far as life experience went. She frowned at the preoccupied expression on his face, aching for that glorious smile of his to revisit the sternly handsome features even though she'd intuited that such smiles were probably incredibly rare.

'Pleased to meet you, Karen.' Sean stepped back with a grin as Gray indicated he wanted his help in taking the old sofa outside. 'I've seen you round the town and sometimes walking the hills or down by the sea. How do you like it out here? Not too lonely for you?'

'I like it just fine, Sean. The peace and quiet is just what I need.'

'Are you going to stand round all day chatting to Miss Ford, or are you going to give me a hand like I asked you to?' Scowling at the younger man, Gray picked up one end of the old sofa and waited with barely concealed impatience for him to lift the other.

'I suppose I'm going to help you, boss—that's why I'm here, isn't it? But it's a sad day when a man can't take the time to share a few words with a new neighbour, don't you think?'

This gently amused remark elicited another dark scowl from Gray, and as the two men passed Karen with the sofa Sean gave her a conspiratorial wink.

Biting her lip to keep from grinning, Karen followed them outside again. 'Shall I make some tea?'

'Got any coffee?' Gray came back.

Tucking her hair behind her ears, Karen felt her cheeks burn at the sudden intense inspection he subjected her to. She personally thought such interested scrutiny was ill-deserved when she was wearing her second oldest pair of jeans and a plain, too-big lilac shirt that had lost a couple of its buttons.

'Sure. How do you take it?'

'Black and strong, no sugar,' came the clipped reply.

Karen nodded. She should have guessed. It probably

summed up the way Gray lived his life, she thought. No frills, just the basic essentials. Milk and sugar would have been far too much of an indulgence for such a man.

'And you, Sean?'

'Tea for me, darlin'…plenty of milk and three sugars.'

'Okay—and how about a slice of home-made fruitcake to go with it?'

'I'm a sucker for home-made cake any time, so I'll say yes, please!' Sean winked at her.

'And you, Mr O'Connell?'

She'd deliberately kept her address formal, so he wouldn't think she was being forward, but there was a maddening twinkle in his eyes as he replied, 'You clearly know how to tempt a man, Miss Ford.'

'Refreshments coming right up, then.' Blushing and smiling shyly, Karen turned back into the house to put the kettle on.

Altogether Gray had brought her a sofa, two matching armchairs in the same tasteful natural linen, and a couple of Victorian brass table-lamps that complemented the traditional interior of the cottage so well that Karen could have hugged him with delight. The new furniture transformed the place. Now all she needed to do was apply a couple of coats of paint to the walls and window frames and it would resemble a home again, rather than a place haunted by the twin ghosts of sadness and neglect.

Taking a sip of tea from a pink mug labelled 'Primadonna'—a long-ago gift from Ryan—she surveyed the two men currently gracing the new armchairs.

Sean had the ease and careless body language of his youth, and was oblivious to anything but the enjoyment of his sweet milky tea, while Gray… Well, Gray was another matter entirely, Karen thought. The long legs clad in close-fitting black jeans seemed almost too long for the chair he sat in. He'd rolled the sleeves of his rust-coloured shirt halfway up his forearms, revealing strong limbs with a distinct smattering of fine dark hair. The fingers that curved round his blue china mug were long and slender, and definitely hinted at artistic leanings. But, unlike Sean, he *wasn't* at ease. His handsome face seemed singularly distant and preoccupied, barely concealing the fact that he was scarcely comfortable with the situation at all and would probably much rather be anywhere else but there.

Was it her? Karen couldn't help wondering if he was regretting that explosive hungry kiss they'd shared last night. Maybe she should bring the matter up? Tell him that it meant nothing and suggest they start again on a more businesslike footing? *Yeah, right.* She could just imagine how that little suggestion would be received. He'd probably laugh mockingly and tell her to grow up.

With a sudden ache in her heart, she smoothed down an imaginary crease in her shirt, then almost choked on her tea when she caught Gray studying her with indisputable heat in his eyes—heat that scorched her even when there was a distance of a good three or four feet between them.

'It was good of you to replace the old furniture,' she said quickly. 'It's nice and cosy now.'

'I should have done it a long time ago,' Gray replied, unsmiling. 'Anything else you can think of that you'd like?'

Karen's fingers tightened round her mug of tea. Unable to meet his gaze just then, because his question had elicited a rather *risqué* response in her brain, she jerked her head vaguely towards the windows. 'I was going to ask if I could give the walls and window frames a fresh coat of paint. I'll buy it myself. I'm a dab hand with a paintbrush.'

'Sure, I'd be happy to come up and do the job for you myself, darlin',' Sean piped up, blue eyes wide as he contemplated the unknowingly stirring picture Karen made with her long slender legs encased in tight faded denim and her waist-length honey-gold hair tumbling freely over her shoulders in the plain lilac blouse that she managed to elevate to 'classy' just because she was wearing it. 'Sure, I could even get you the paint. What do you say, boss?' The younger man glanced at Gray, whose unsmiling countenance appeared immediately forbidding.

'If anyone's going to paint this house it will be me,' he said tersely, his aloof glance clearly berating Sean for imagining anything else.

'I don't want to put you to any trouble.' Fielding the surge of embarrassment that flooded her, Karen folded her arms uncomfortably. Of course she hadn't expected her landlord to offer to come and do the job himself. She suddenly wished she had just gone ahead and done it and suffered the consequences afterwards if he really didn't like it.

She watched Gray get up and stalk to the small galley kitchen to rinse out his mug. When he came out again he walked straight to the front door and wrenched it wide. 'I'll be back around ten tomorrow to make a start,' he said and disappeared outside.

Karen exhaled a long slow breath.

Amused, Sean got to his feet, leaving his mug and plate on the coffee table.

'Don't let him get to you, darlin'. Sure, his bark is worse than his bite. And, by the way, that cake was out of this world. The best I've ever tasted and I'm not joking. I couldn't trouble you for a slice to take home, could I? My sister Liz runs a café with all kinds of home-made fare, and I'd like her to try it.'

'Of course. Just give me a minute and I'll wrap some up for you.'

She was back almost straight away with the promised cake, and after thanking her, then winking at her for a second time, the young man left the cottage with a cheerful whistle.

* * *

As a waft of fresh paint floated through the air and assailed her nostrils, Karen stepped out of the kitchen to watch Gray as he crouched low to tackle the skirting. This morning he was again dressed from head to foot in black, his longish hair gleaming even more darkly than his clothing, and as her covetous glance surveyed him Karen knew the most compelling urge to touch him…to make him turn around…to make him notice her. She was beginning to feel frustrated beyond belief that his aloofness seemed to be growing rather than diminishing, and something inside her wanted to try and coax him back to the land of the living—which was quite ironic when she contemplated her own desire for isolation. Still, one step at a time…

'Why don't I give you a hand?' she asked, her voice faltering despite her need to sound confident.

The paintbrush stilled in Gray's hand. Carefully wiping the drips on the inside of the paint can, then laying the brush across it, he looked up to meet her gaze. Karen's heart took a slow elevator ride to her stomach.

'I prefer to get along on my own,' was the slow but succinct answer she received.

She wasn't surprised, but when curiosity and downright foolhardiness got the better part of common sense, she folded her arms across the orange tie-dyed tee shirt she wore, willing herself not to flinch beneath that cool-as-a-cucumber gaze of his that would surely freeze out even the most dogged admirer?

'Why is it that you prefer to do everything on your own?'

'Does that bother you?' He looked directly into her eyes.

Every cell in Karen's body seemed to vibrate with heat. Flustered, she shook her head, wishing she'd never started this. Why couldn't she just have stayed put in the kitchen, making her scones?

'No. I mean yes. If I'm honest, it *does* bother me. No man is an island. We all need a bit of help and support from time to time.'

'That why you hide yourself out here on your own?' Gray probed, getting to his feet.

Nervously moistening her lips with her tongue, Karen swallowed hard. His immediately interested glance caught the movement and turned from ice to fire in less than a second. Her knees buckled.

'I wasn't talking about me.'

'What if I told you I *wanted* to talk about you?'

Somehow his voice had acquired a hypnotic resonance that sent goosebumps scudding across Karen's skin like out-of-control wildfire. It was all she could do to keep herself from crossing her legs, because the sensation at her innermost core was suddenly hotly, sweetly, demandingly sexual.

'What do you want to know about me?' The question left her lips in a hoarse whisper.

'I want to know if you have a sense of adventure, Karen… or are you the type of woman who likes to play safe?'

'I don't know what you mean.' Her gaze lowered, because the expression in his eyes was too hot for her to handle just then. It was having the same effect as a branding iron held too close to her skin.

'You know damn well exactly what I mean.' A dark eyebrow quirked upwards towards his brow.

All the blood seemed to rush to Karen's head. Inside her chest, her heart throbbed like some heavy tribal drumbeat that she couldn't make stop, even as her nipples grew almost unbearably achy and hard. If he could do this to her body—make her ache and want and need just with words—what effect would his touch have? Recalling his fierce, bruising kiss the other night, she already knew the answer. There was no question he would set her on fire.

'I don't think you should be asking me such personal questions.' Completely out of her depth, Karen went to turn away, her wary blue eyes widening in shock when Gray gripped her upper arm in a vice and spun her back towards him.

'Don't you? Then stop coming on to me with those coy little-girl looks of yours. You have no idea what you're getting yourself into…*none*.'

Wrenching her arm free, Karen rubbed it with resentment and hurt. 'I'm not coming on to you! You really flatter yourself, don't you?'

He gave her a maddeningly knowing little smile. 'Go back to your baking, sweetheart. If you're good…or maybe I should say *bad*…I'll come and tell you later about a particular erotic fantasy of mine about women in the kitchen.'

'No, thanks.' Humiliated and indignant, Karen tossed her head and beat a hasty retreat.

'I never had you down as a coward!' Gray called after her, chuckling out loud.

Karen put her head round the door and glared back at him, blue eyes sparking like a firecracker. 'And I *definitely* had you down as a sadist,' she retorted angrily, her jaw aching with the effort of restraining her fury. 'Sadly, I haven't been proved wrong yet!'

'Now you've really hurt my feelings.' Affecting an expression of pained disappointment, then grinning like a schoolboy, triumphant at getting the last word, he dropped down onto his haunches to resume his painting…

CHAPTER FOUR

IT HAD started raining again, and Karen's restlessness grew. Gray was striding in and out from the van, oblivious to the downpour, clearing away dustsheets and decorating implements, evidently not the least bit inclined to attempt conversation of any kind. What was wrong with the man, for goodness' sake? Apart from his humiliating accusation earlier, about her trying to come on to him, he hadn't said another word. Every time she'd dared put her head round the door to see how he was doing, he'd been diligently painting, moving the thick paintbrush up and down the wall with sure smooth strokes that were fascinating to observe. It had made Karen wonder what he looked like when he was creating *real* works of art.

Sighing, she filled the kettle and put it on to boil. When in doubt, make tea—or in Gray's case strong black *coffee*. But whether he intended to stay or go Karen would have to wait and see.

Bending down to the oven, she withdrew the tray of newly baked scones, her mouth watering at the tantalising smell they exuded. Picking them gingerly off the tray one by one, she laid them on the wire rack on the worktop to cool, gratified at the way they had turned out—faintly golden on the outside and hopefully moist and soft inside. Just the way she liked them. Unable to resist, she broke one in half and, blowing on it briefly, popped a small wedge into her mouth.

'Mmm—delicious! Even if I do say so myself.'

As the cake melted on her tongue, Karen genuinely sa-voured it. She had always loved her food, and wasn't ashamed to admit it. It was one of life's greatest pleasures. Akin to reading a good book, listening to a beautiful piece of music or making love…

'They look good.'

She nearly jumped out of her skin as she glanced guiltily round to find Gray leaning against the door jamb, his face and hair glistening from the rain, a teasing smile on his lips that made her feel like a child caught with her hand in the cookie jar.

'Would you like one? I was just going to make some tea… or coffee if you prefer?' Wiping her hand across her lips, she prayed there weren't any betraying crumbs in evidence.

'Coffee would be good.'

'I'll get you a towel first. You're wet through.' Flustered, Karen moved to slide past him. The doorway was narrow, to say the least, and Gray, with his tall broad-shouldered phy-sique all but filled it.

He didn't move. All of a sudden she found herself wedged between his chest and the door jamb. The damp warmth of his sweater pressed provocatively against her breasts in the thin tee shirt, and she knew with a little zing of panic that he had no intention of letting her pass.

'I…I…'

Her senses were overwhelmed. Assaulted by the fresh, clean outdoorsy smell of his clothes, the faint woody tang of his cologne and the provocative testosterone-laden scent of the man himself, she felt an answering tremor wing its way through her body, bringing an aroused flush to her cheeks and a soft, discernible tremble to her lips.

Raising her eyes, Karen gazed up into a deep silvery-grey ocean—a wild, storm-tossed sea on a cloudy day—and knew

that she was irrevocably captured...a willing prisoner with no
desire or even the remotest urge to escape. At that moment she
was right where she wanted to be. Just then she could pretend
she was once again a woman with no troubled past or uncertain future, because only the arousing present existed, with
its tangible heat thrumming like a silent steady current between herself and Gray. And suddenly the little old-fashioned
kitchen, with its warm, homely smell of freshly baked scones
and a faint, musky dampness from old stone walls seemed
like the most romantic, intoxicating place on earth.

With one long lean finger Gray traced the delicate line of
her jaw, his touch electrifying her, making her pupils dilate,
causing her breath to still for a second while her heartbeat
raced hard, like an athlete towards the finishing line. She'd
never known it was possible to desire anyone so much until
even the mere thought of them could make her want to give
him body and soul without a care. *Why hadn't she felt that
way about Ryan?* Guilt consumed her at the thought. He'd
given her everything, yet she had definitely kept something
back from him...a vital, important, passionate part of herself
that needed expression—and not just through her writing or
performing.

'Gray, I—'

'Don't talk,' he ordered, eyes widening as if suddenly
coming out of a trance. 'Just let me look at you.'

And he did. Gray's artist's eye scrutinised her face, noting
the exquisitely aligned features with silent but fierce appreciation. Her beautiful blue eyes were her most beguiling asset, he
thought, deep and sensual and almost almond-shaped, with
fine curling lashes—the kind of eyes that surely most men
would willingly drown in. His gaze moved up a little to the
smooth dark blonde wing of her brows, then back down to
the small elegant slope of her nose and the prettily contoured

mouth, with its sultry full lower lip, pink and plump, bereft of lipstick and just begging to be kissed.

In less than an instant blood rushed to the core of Gray's manhood, and he wanted her as he wanted his next breath. But he didn't give in to the almost overwhelming urge to plunder and ravish because he knew a sudden, much greater desire to tease and provoke and sensually savour. He'd make the pretty widow want him so badly that every thought of her husband and any other man she had been romantically involved with would be wiped clean out of her head. Only then would he allow himself to take what they both so desperately wanted. And when they did succumb to the desire that was shimmering between them, like an oasis in one-hundred-and-twenty-degree heat, it would need more than a whole fire brigade to put out the conflagration.

For Karen, it took a few seconds longer for reality to sink in. When she realised Gray had no intention of doing anything more than just looking at her, instead of winding his arms around her waist as she needed him to—as she *ached* for him to—she let her hands drop redundantly down by her sides and dipped her head. It hurt to know that he desired her but wasn't prepared to do anything about it. What was it about her that put him off? Did he think she came with too much baggage? Was that it? Did he imagine that she would want much more than just an intense physical fling?

She suddenly wished that Ryan was around, so that she could ask him what was the best thing to do, then realised how preposterous the notion was. This was one situation that she was going to have to sort out for herself. Wherever he was, Ryan would only want what was best for Karen—the outcome that would cause her the least pain. Somehow she knew that, as far as Gray O'Connell was concerned, on some level she'd already signed up for a truckload of that particular commodity.

'Hey...' His fingers sliding beneath her jaw, he tilted her chin to align her glance with his.

It was amazing how many shades of silver-grey there were in his pupils, Karen mused with wonder. She hadn't realised how varied the colour could be.

'I think I'd like to paint you,' he said.

Karen felt a little throb of panic at the idea. 'A portrait, you mean?'

'A life study.'

'You mean without—without clothes?' She couldn't prevent the tremor in her voice.

Gray smiled as if her flustered confusion amused him. 'Most life studies are nude,' he told her evenly. 'Does that bother you?'

'Not generally, no. But me posing for one definitely does.'

'Live a little, Karen. Isn't that what you'd really like to do?'

How many times had she promised herself that very thing? She was only twenty-six, for goodness' sake! Was she going to spend the rest of her life in recrimination and regret? *Ryan would turn in his grave.* But, just the same, she had to live a little by degrees. Becoming an artist's model for this aloof, enigmatic man—posing without clothes on to boot—was too much to expect in too short a time. Even if she *was* craving his attention a little too much for her peace of mind.

'I'm not the kind of person who can easily throw caution to the wind,' she started to explain, going alternately hot and cold beneath Gray's laserlike glance, because she had nowhere to hide when he looked at her like that. 'I'm—'

She tried to summon up words that would adequately describe how she felt about exposing her body without sounding like a complete prude. She'd performed on stage to audiences varying from small to large, yet she was innately shy. Apart from her jeans, her clothes were generally soft and free-flowing, rarely tight or figure-hugging. Even Ryan had teased her about her reticence to show off her figure.

'Repressed?' Gray suggested softly, his gaze lingering with deliberate provocation on her mouth.

'No. I wouldn't say I was repressed.' Her face aflame, Karen tried again to pass the man who was holding her prisoner with just a look, and gasped out loud when he caught hold of her arm and pressed her back up against the door jamb.

The kettle whistled to indicate it had boiled. Outside the rain beat a steady tattoo against the windows. The sharp intoxicating scent of fresh paint wafted in from the sitting room, and Karen began to wish that Gray had just got straight in the van and gone after he'd packed up his things.

His intimate interrogation was beginning to make her squirm with unease. It was one thing longing for him to kiss her—quite another allowing him to put her under the microscope as if she was some interesting dissection. But then, what was she supposed to do, when her body was so over-stimulated and yet languorous with need at the same time? What those mystifying eyes were doing to her body would tempt the most devout celibate to give up their vows.

She was helpless to disguise the intensely intimate reaction of her body. Inside her white lace bra her nipples surged and hardened into prickling distended buds, making her squirm in embarrassment as she realised Gray had seen immediately what had happened. His pupils darkened to fierce midnight. Whatever Karen was feeling he was feeling it too…maybe even more so.

'You'd better go get me that towel, Miss Ford, before I succumb to a temptation that it's becoming increasingly painful to resist.' He let go of her arm with a scowl as her brows knit in confusion.

'Why? Does that worry you?'

'You're not like any of the other women I've known.' His face contorted in a flash of anger. 'You're basically a very decent, loving woman, Karen. You need a man who's the same. Not some dark-souled outsider like me. I'm afraid if I touch you I might never want to stop—and then where would we be?'

His lips twisted in a mocking little smile that caused Karen untold agony, and because she couldn't think of a single thing to say that would persuade him differently, she scooted past him and fled into the bathroom. As she selected a fluffy white towel from the airing cupboard, she pressed it close to her cheek for a moment. Staring into the square wooden-framed mirror above the sink, she saw with a shock the physical effect Gray O'Connell was having on her.

Her blue eyes were dilated and sparkling, and there was a hectic flush to her skin that made it appear as if she'd just stumbled out of bed after a night of pure, unrestrained passion. Had she ever looked like that after a night with Ryan? Of course she must have! She'd just never noticed it, that was all. Skimming her hand along the side of her cheek, Karen discovered her skin was as hot to the touch as it appeared. She was all but burning up. Even her pulse was still racing. And all because of her shocking attraction to her infuriating landlord.

Frustration and anger throbbed simultaneously through her, and she wished again that she possessed some of the necessary sophistication that would help her be more appealing to the man she desired. If only she didn't look younger than her age. If only she could beguile him with wit and warmth and irresistible charm. *If only she didn't have her heart in her eyes every time she so much as glanced at him.*

Clutching the towel to her chest, she opened the door of the tiny narrow bathroom, with its old-fashioned claw-footed bath, and returned to the kitchen.

Gray was leaning against the door jamb where she had
left him, his handsome face preoccupied. Handing him the
towel, Karen slid past him without a backwards glance. She
saw straight away that he'd turned off the kettle and moved
it to a back burner on the cooker, and she tried not to mind
that he wouldn't stay for coffee if she asked. It was obvious
that he was eager to get out of there as soon as possible, and
she bit her lip to stifle the tears that kept threatening. She
was determined to keep them at bay at least until he'd gone.
To distract herself, she selected half a dozen scones from the
wire rack where they'd been left to cool and popped them into
a plastic sandwich bag. She held them out to Gray with an
uncertain little smile and prayed she looked more composed
than she felt. Yes, she desired Gray O'Connell, but she didn't
want to make herself totally vulnerable to him. Only a fool
would do that.

He stopped drying his hair with the towel and stared at her.

'I thought you might like to take some of my baking home,'
she said softly.

When he made no move to take the scones, but continued
to examine her with an expression she was beyond explaining
right then, Karen shrugged her shoulders and put the bag on
the worktop.

'Even if you don't want them, maybe Chase might like
them? I've made too many and they don't keep.'

'One kiss,' he said hoarsely, and threw the towel on the
worktop.

Startled, Karen was still gathering her wits as he stepped
towards her and hauled her roughly up against his chest. The
sensation of heat and damp from his sweater enveloped her,
even as the wild fresh scent of the sea and the Atlantic air
invaded her senses so profoundly that she suddenly felt dizzy
as well as exhilarated. As Gray bent his head to kiss her she
didn't have even the remotest inclination to protest. Instead,

her lips parted easily as his mouth lowered with unstoppable urgency and took hungry, greedy possession of hers.

She tasted heat, heartache and desire, all wrapped up in one intense compelling package, as he plundered and took what she so willingly gave, his tongue dipping in and out of her velvet softness like a man possessed, the faint stubble on his angled jaw scraping her chin as his hands slid down to her bottom and impelled her hips hard into his own. Shaking with need, Karen kissed him back with soft little moans that seemed to leave her throat without her realisation. She was near mindless with wanting, and she no longer wished for sophistication—simply ached in every muscle and limb for the fire they had stoked between them to be sated.

Then, as suddenly and abruptly as he had pulled her into his arms, Gray released her, his hands gripping her by her shoulders to hold her away from him. The next instant he abruptly let her go and, dazed, Karen stumbled, hitting her lower back against the worktop. She stared at him as pain and humiliation hazed her eyes, her lips still throbbing from his hungry kisses, her body languid with the desire he'd stoked, and at an utter loss to know what to do or say.

'Are you okay?' He voiced his concern almost grudgingly, as if he couldn't wait to be gone.

Karen suddenly wanted him gone, too. Now she understood why hate and love were so closely intertwined.

'Why should you care?' she tried, but was unable to prevent the sob that accompanied her words.

'I *do* care, damn you!'

Shaking her head, Karen blinked up at him through eyes that were helplessly brimming with tears. 'No, you don't. Just go. Please…just go.'

His lips pressed grimly together, Gray turned and did just as she asked…

* * *

Wiping his palette knife clean of the worst excesses of paint, Gray laid it carefully down beside the black metal box of paints. The sun filtered in through the huge uncurtained window, pouring light onto the picture fastened to his easel. The rough sketch was of a woman with long rippling gold hair and almond-shaped blue eyes that gazed back at him with hurt as well as temptation in their depths. *Karen*.

He hadn't been able to think about anything else since he'd left her crying in the kitchen of his father's old cottage. That had been two weeks ago. He'd made no attempt to get in touch in all that time. He wondered what she'd been doing. He hadn't seen her on the beach or in the woods—not that she would have welcomed bumping into him. She'd probably chalked him up to bitter experience by now. It was nothing less than he deserved, but still a pain twisted through his guts, making him scowl.

Cursing out loud, he raked his fingers through his already mussed black hair, then reached out to tear the rough portrait from the easel. In spite of himself his fingertips lingered on the likeness he had created, smoothing down the soft curve of the feminine cheekbone he had captured only too well, despite having to work from memory only. But there it was. Karen's face was indelibly printed on Gray's mind like a photograph he couldn't erase.

The door of his studio creaked open just then, and Chase padded hopefully across the bare wooden floor and nudged his head into Gray's side. His master glanced down distract-edly at the huge dog, absent-mindedly stroking the impressive fawn head.

'Give me half an hour, hmm? Then I'll take you for your walk.'

As if understanding perfectly, Chase turned round, loped back across the floor and went out through the door.

Replacing the unfinished sketch of Karen on the easel,

Gray exited the large sunlit room that was bereft of heating or adornment of any kind, except for the haphazard stacks of paintings propped up against two of the walls. Without realising why, he found himself hurrying downstairs to the first-floor landing.

In the middle of the largest bedroom in the house was a beautiful handcrafted bed, with a plain navy blue throw flung across the duvet. Apart from the sensually coloured Moroccan rug on the floor next to the bed, there was one large chest of drawers in reclaimed pine, and two cherrywood bedside cabinets, but that was it as far as furnishings and fittings went. No curtains or blinds hung at the windows, and right now, as the sunlight hit the bare wooden boards of the floor, highlighting the dust-motes dancing in its beam, the room appeared almost stark in its emptiness. But Gray paid no mind to that. Stalking across the floor, he pulled open one of the drawers in the pine chest and took out a faded brown envelope.

Dropping down onto the huge bed, he shook out the contents onto the navy blue throw. Three photographs lay face upwards on the bed. He picked up the first one that caught his eye and held it up to examine it more closely. It was Maura, with her pale blonde hair and laughing green eyes. They'd started an affair when Gray was working in London, and she'd stubbornly followed him back to Ireland—even though he'd tried to end it between them—and somehow moved in. He'd been glad of her company then. She'd been with him when Paddy had died and things had been pretty bleak. Just knowing someone else was in the house had helped, because he'd ultimately been terrified of facing himself. Now he wondered how she'd stuck it. If Gray had been morose before, he'd been worse after the tragedy of his father's death.

For six months after it had happened he'd become a virtual recluse. He'd never meant for that to happen. Somehow he'd withdrawn so far into himself that he'd known he wasn't fit company for anyone—let alone a bright, vivacious woman with a bold laugh and a love of life he couldn't possibly begin to emulate. So he'd lock himself in his studio, where he would paint into the early hours until he was grey-faced and frozen, only leaving the room to use the bathroom or grab a bite to eat. He hadn't cared what—it might as well have been cardboard for all he'd been able to taste of it. He had grown numb to everything. His heart, his mind, his senses had all been frozen.

Maura had been more or less left to her own devices—but she was a resourceful woman, who'd forged a successful career in the still mainly male-dominated world of investment banking, so she wasn't exactly short of determination or grit.

Surprisingly, she had made herself a life of sorts in Gray's once fashionable, still beautiful old house, and had started to interest herself in restoring it to its former glory. In the process she had involved herself in the life of the community—making friends with shopkeepers, publicans and neighbours alike—and had generally been well thought of. *Until her less than discreet dalliances with some of the local lads had come under scrutiny, that was.* Gray had eventually got wind of the gossip that was circulating like wildfire in the small close-knit community, but he hadn't actually cared very much. Not then. He'd reacted by immersing himself even further in his painting, and when on occasion he'd found himself in need of some intimate companionship Maura had still been a willing and enthusiastic lover.

He shook his head now at how crazy things had got. How low, how dark, how plain bloody miserable...

When Mike Hogan, his best friend from university, had shown up out of the blue, begging a bed for a week or so before he jetted off to Canada and a new job, Maura had immediately set her sights on him. And who could have blamed her? Mike was pleasant-looking, witty, intelligent—and, more to the point, a far more sociable creature than Gray could ever hope to be. Within a couple of days of setting eyes on each other the pair had been making plans to leave together.

'You're welcome to each other,' Gray muttered darkly, then tore the photograph cleanly straight down the middle and dropped the two glossy halves carelessly on the bed—something he should have done a long time ago.

The second photograph was an old black-and-white print of his mother, and his heart lurched as he studied it.

A pretty woman, she was smiling tenderly down at the dark-haired baby she held in her arms as if he were her sun, her moon, her stars. It was himself as a baby. Only Gray thought if she had really loved him that much, why had she chosen to end her life and leave him when he was only three? He'd never found out the truth about why she'd committed suicide. Paddy had kept stubbornly silent about Niamh O'Connell's reasons for doing such a shocking thing, and in his heart Gray had started to blame him for her death. It had tainted their already poor relationship.

Swallowing down the painful swell inside his throat, Gray put the photograph carefully back into the envelope.

The last print was a colour photograph of Paddy himself. It had been taken on a jaunt with some locals by none other than Eileen Kennedy, the shopkeeper-cum-postmistress. He was standing on a hillock, a bottle of Guinness held aloft, and a devilish grin splitting his mouth wide. It had been taken just three months before he'd died. Probably around the same time that Gray had found out that his last investment had helped his portfolio run into millions… *Poor comfort the knowledge had brought him.*

It finally dawned on him that it was the journey he'd loved—the wheeling, dealing and speculating that had lit his fire—*not* the actual destination. Money hadn't impressed his

father and why should it have when the pursuit of it had taken
his only son too far away from him?

'Wherever you are, I hope you're happy, you old devil.'
He addressed the picture with a painfully rueful smile, then
relegated the photograph—along with the bittersweet memory
of his father—back to the confines of the brown envelope.

Downstairs again, Gray pulled on his battered leather jacket,
speared a hand through his already ruffled black hair and
whistled up Chase to go for a walk. He deliberately headed
for the beach, thinking that the sea air would do him good,
blow away the proverbial cobwebs, and help him think more
clearly. Looking at the photographs, delving into his past,
hadn't helped. He'd known it wouldn't before he'd even un-
dertaken the exercise. Sometimes sheer bloody-mindedness
just got the better of him.

Anyhow, now there was a tight band of tension round his
head and it served him right. He was too bloody destructive
for his own good sometimes.

Relaxation—if he'd ever really given house-room to such
a concept—was a thing of the past. Now all he seemed to do
was spend every day regretting more and more the bad deci-
sions he'd made and punishing himself with the memories.

Not exactly the best way to live a life, he thought. Still,
as he climbed the hillock that led down to the vast strand of
white sandy beach it was his beautiful fair-haired tenant that
predominantly occupied his mind—not the perpetual inner
turmoil that seemed to accompany his every waking moment.
Just what the hell was he going to do about this persistent
dangerous fascination he had for her? A fascination that had
crept up on him and taken too strong a hold before he had
time to avert it?

She didn't deserve a man as inwardly craggy as him.
She deserved better…much better. But even so Gray's heart

suddenly seemed to beat more strongly in his chest just at the mere possibility that he might see Karen again sometime soon, and there was a rare spring in his step as he increased his stride to catch up with Chase...

CHAPTER FIVE

KAREN answered the door with a crazy leap of hope in her heart—only to have it recede with bitter disappointment and surprise when she found Sean, Gray's young assistant from a couple of weeks ago, standing on the step. Blinking up at him in the strong morning sunlight, she shivered at the cold gust of air that also greeted her, wondering why he had come and if Gray had sent him. She knew she was probably clutching at straws but, having not seen the man for a fortnight, she was beginning to feel a little frayed around the edges.

Sean grinned and Karen waited for him to speak first, still nursing the vain hope that he was bringing news of Gray.

'Hello, there.'

He was wearing a short denim jacket faded to the palest blue over a once black tee shirt now almost grey. With his long legs encased in similar light blue denims, he had the lazily optimistic grace of youth and his fair share of beauty, too—making Karen feel a sudden deep pang for the lost innocence of her own youth. For a moment she gazed up at his boyishly handsome face, with its unruly halo of uncombed fair hair and clear blue eyes, and wished somehow that she could be more like him. She knew it might be an unfair assumption, but he really did look as if he didn't have a care in the world on that bright blustery morning. She couldn't help but envy that.

Yet his appearance still engendered a heaviness of heart, because he wasn't the man she'd been hoping to find standing there. Instinctively she knew that Gray was deliberately keeping his distance. If he'd wanted her to get the message that this craziness between them wasn't going to progress any further then she'd received it loud and clear. For two weeks now she'd hardly been able to sleep nights for thoughts of him. It was crazy and futile, but she seemed powerless to put a stop to it. And Karen would bet her last penny that he hadn't suffered similarly sleepless nights over *her*.

If only she'd been able to deal with their attraction a little better. If only she had some knowledge of the rules of this game maybe she could have handled things with a bit more finesse instead of feeling so painfully lost. Maybe then she wouldn't have scared him off the way she'd done. But she couldn't turn back the clock and be something she wasn't. All she could do was deal with what was right in front of her—and right now life had brought Sean, with his twinkling blue eyes and ready smile. The least she could do was greet him in a civil manner.

'Hello.' She smiled back, genuinely taken aback to see the flicker of pleasure in his face that her greeting had provoked.

'Karen,' he replied in a rush, reddening slightly, 'I was wondering if you wouldn't mind taking a walk with me?'

'A walk, Sean?' She resisted the wild impulse to giggle. His request seemed so incongruous that Karen's interest was snagged in spite of herself.

'Yes. You like walking, don't you?' He looped his fingers behind the black leather belt fastened round his worn blue denims and managed to look sheepish and endearing all at once.

Wiping her hands carefully on the checked tea towel she'd been drying the dishes with, Karen frowned. As endearing as the young Irishman appeared, she really didn't feel like going anywhere just now. Her mood was a little too blue, for one thing. It was the result of another sleepless night over Gray O'Connell, along with sadness and guilt because suddenly she couldn't seem to remember her husband's face any more.

'Of course I like walking. But I'm—I'm rather busy just now, Sean.'

'I thought you might say that.' Running a hand around the back of his neck, he glanced down at the grass verge just to the side of him. Then, to Karen's surprise, he seemed to regroup himself. He lifted his chin, then gazed directly into her eyes once more, as if reaching a decision.

'I've seen you walking on the beach from time to time. You're always alone. I thought that if you were going that way today you might like some company.'

'That's very sweet of you, Sean, but I—'

'Don't think I'm coming on to you or anything like that— not that I wouldn't mind, if you see what I mean…' He shifted awkwardly from one foot to the other, momentarily ill at ease. 'But I've got something to ask you about. Will you come for a walk so that we can discuss it?'

'You mean now?' Karen glanced over her shoulder at the spick and span sitting room, with its new coat of paint and the smart new furniture that had immediately revived the cottage's previously careworn appearance. She'd just spent the morning cleaning the place to within an inch of its life. The comforting smell of polish floated up from the furniture surfaces she had vigorously shined, and the black iron grate round the fire positively gleamed from her enthusiastic administrations. The stack of washing up from her baking had been done, and her latest batch of bread and buns lay cooling on wire racks on the worktop.

Baking…

She did it because it was an outlet for the creativity she

wasn't expressing through her music and it helped to pass the time. But because she didn't have a freezer on the premises nearly half of her baking ended up in the bin. It was a shame, but she wasn't exactly on friendly enough terms with anyone in town or thereabouts to give it away. Something she would have done willingly. Even Gray hadn't taken the scones she'd offered him that day. But then the atmosphere between them had been so tense that it was understandable he'd left without taking them.

Unconsciously her teeth worried at her lip. *Why shouldn't she go for a walk with the amiable Sean?* She would have gone anyway at some point this afternoon. Staying in the house for a whole day without venturing outside would hardly help her melancholy mood, whereas a walk just might.

'It's a fine day. All you have to do is put some shoes on and get your coat.' Glancing down at Karen's feet, Sean saw with amusement that they were bare. Pink coral-painted toenails and all.

'All right, then.' Caving in to his undoubtedly natural charm, Karen stepped back from the door with her cheeks suddenly as pink as her toenails.

Acting spontaneously was not something she was used to, and it caused her more anguish than it ought to. It made her aware that she still had a lot to learn as far as loosening up a little went. Still, today she would make the effort to be different. Sean was likeable, and seemed trustworthy. And Gray had employed him, so he must be okay.

Throwing down the tea towel onto the nearest chair, she stooped down to the shoe stand behind the door to get her walking boots. Rescuing the thick yellow socks that were stuffed inside, she took them over to the armchair to put them on.

'Don't stand outside, Sean. Come in. I won't be a minute.'

Stepping inside, Sean glanced interestedly round, his nostrils twitching. 'Something smells good—and I don't mean the polish.'

'I've been baking.' Karen grinned up at him through her mane of silky honey hair as she bent to do up her laces.

'Sure, you're a dangerous woman, Miss Ford. What is it this time? Another delicious fruitcake?' Sean volleyed her grin with one of his own, momentarily transfixed by the sight of her loveliness and all that glorious long hair.

'I've been baking bread and making buns,' she answered.

'Well, it's good to know that you like cooking.'

'Why?' Laughter bubbling up inside her, Karen pushed to her feet, tugging the hem of the blue chambray shirt she was wearing tidily down over the waistband of her jeans.

'My mother's always said it's a useful skill to have—for a woman or a man. Are you ready?'

For answer, she lifted her thick sheepskin coat off the peg and slipped her arms into it. It was amazing how a little human contact and humour could change one's mood for the better, she thought, feeling herself warm towards the boyish Sean even more.

'Ready as I'll ever be. Lead the way.' She stood back as he passed her, catching the scent of a spicy cologne that was a little too overpowering, and wondered briefly if he was wearing it for her benefit. Then, dismissing the thought as too silly for words, she followed him outside.

Despite her previously downbeat mood, her spirits lifted almost instantly as she breathed in the brisk fresh air that blew her hair into a wild burnished gold cloud behind her head. The wild and stormy weather never failed to make her fiercely glad that she'd come to this place. A place she now almost regarded as home.

* * *

'So you've lived round here all your life?' Karen dug her hands into the deep pockets of her sheepskin as she walked beside Sean, vainly trying to keep up with his long-legged stride across the beach.

'I have. I like it well enough.'

He flashed a smile that Karen was certain must make the local girls light up like neon when it was trained on them.

'How about yourself, Karen? Where are you from?'

'A suburb of London. It has its advantages, living there, but often I yearned for some peace and quiet. If I was from here I couldn't ever envisage wanting to live anywhere else.'

Her announcement was passionate because it came from the heart. Glancing up at the cloudless azure sky, at the gulls circling above them with their coarse shrieking cries, she felt a definite sense of rightness roll over her. There wasn't anywhere else on earth she'd rather be right now. Her gaze moved down along the vast stretch of empty beach that lay before them, with the sea lapping relatively calmly at its edge today, and she wondered how she could bear going home to England again. Wondered, too, if the day would come when she would even *want* to. This place was her idea of heaven.

If only she had someone to share it with. She didn't mean right now, because Sean was amiable enough company for sure. She meant someone to share it with permanently. *Someone like Gray O'Connell.* The dangerous thought slammed into her hard, making her throat ache and her heart race. Not seeing him for two whole weeks had begun to feel like an eternity. What was he doing? Was he seeing someone else? Was that why he'd been so angry and so eager to leave that day when he'd finished the decorating? Did he feel torn because he was attracted to her when there was already another person in his life? Her stomach cramped with jealousy at the idea. Why did just the thought of him with someone else hurt so much? It didn't make sense. None of this crazy obsession she was developing for him made sense. *Surely she couldn't be in her right mind?*

'Karen?'

'Sean?' She came to a standstill beside the tall young Irishman, blinking up at him as the hauntingly handsome dark face in her mind, with its sculpted cheekbones and glacial eyes, reluctantly receded. Strands of silky blond hair blew across her face in the wind, temporarily shielding her embarrassment at being caught out not paying attention.

'I asked you a question, but you're away in your own little world.'

'I'm sorry.' She screwed up her face in sheepish apology. 'I do that sometimes...space out, I mean. I didn't mean to be rude.'

'No offence taken.' Digging his hands into the pockets of his jeans, Sean looked thoughtful for a moment. 'I was asking if you'd be interested in a bit of a part-time job? I briefly mentioned it to you before. My sister Liz has just opened up a café in town, and she's looking to recruit some help. As soon as she tasted your fruitcake she wanted to meet you.'

Karen frowned in bemusement. Of all the things he might have asked her, offering her a part-time job wasn't the first thing that had naturally sprung to mind. 'A café, you say?'

'Oh, it's not just an ordinary breakfasts and sandwiches sort of place. It's more upmarket than that. Liz has travelled all over the world, you know. It's a themed café...Mexican. She's called it Liz's Cantina. And she doesn't just serve Mexican food... There's cake and all kinds of great desserts, too'

'Your sister has started up a themed café here in town?' Karen grinned from ear to ear. 'What a crazy, wonderful idea!' She'd noticed some building work going on at one of the previously boarded-up buildings just off the main street a while ago, but she'd had no idea what it was being renovated for. She didn't like the idea that she'd been walking round so preoccupied with her own troubled thoughts that she hadn't even noticed what was going on around her.

'You really think so?' Sean stuck the toe of his boot into the sand and gouged a hole.

'Of course I do!' Clasping her hands momentarily to her chest, all of a sudden Karen was inspired by Sean's enterprising sister, whom she hadn't even met yet. She'd never considered the possibility of a part-time job before, but right now it held an almost irresistible appeal. It would get her out of the house more, for one thing, and she would get to meet other people.

'Liz wants to hire someone a bit more worldly than some of the local girls. A bit more "clued up", as she puts it. Will you come and see her? At least have a chat with her about a possible job?'

'When was she thinking of?'

'Later this afternoon? She closes at five, and I usually go round to give her a bit of a hand tidying up. I'll pick you up at about a quarter to, if you like?'

'I suppose I ought to at least go and meet her...thank her for thinking of me. But I have my own car. I can drive myself rather than have you go out of your way to pick me up.'

Karen shrugged a little nervously. It seemed such an ordinary simple thing to do, to go and see someone about a job, but it was actually something she'd never done before. When she'd finished college she'd met Ryan almost straight away, married him, and then started to pursue her singing career. As far as promoting her career, arranging gigs and doing all the accompanying paper and telephone work that had been involved—all of that had been Ryan's domain. He'd taken care of everything. He'd worked in record management for ten years before they'd met, and there wasn't much he hadn't known about the music industry.

She'd depended on him for so much. Had she given enough

back in return? She really hoped so. She was desolate at the idea that maybe she hadn't.

'I'd prefer to pick you up, if you don't mind? Liz has already instructed me, and she'll have my guts for garters if I don't. So...shall we finish our walk, then?' Sean interrupted her wayward thoughts.

Staring out at the shimmering white strand ahead of them, Karen smiled. Tasting the briny tang of the sea spray on her tongue, she vowed not to spoil this unexpected opportunity to enjoy the fresh air and exercise. All in all, today was turning out to be a much better day than she'd anticipated. This morning all she'd had to look forward to was cleaning, baking, and her own solitary company. And for once she'd actually felt scared that it might not be enough. Clearly she wasn't as hardy or as resolved to the isolation of living alone as she'd thought. Certainly nowhere near as hardy and resolved as Gray O'Connell seemed to be...

Shielding his gaze from the fierce glare of the noonday sun, Gray blinked at the two solitary figures some distance away from him on the beach. A gust of wind lifted a lock of black hair from his forehead, and in profile his brows were knit together in stern contemplation. When he realised that one of the figures was Karen his jaw hardened instantly, jealousy jack-knifing through his guts so sharply that he actually took a step back to steady himself. Beside him, Chase chafed at the bit, longing to be allowed to bound up the beach unrestrained like he usually did, but right now his master was holding on to his collar a little too tightly for that wish to become a reality.

'Be still!' Gray's huskily angry voice brooked no argument. Chase hung his great fawn head and looked duly chastised.

But it wasn't the dog that had fuelled his temper. It was the sight of the woman down on the beach that had kindled the flames of his ire. The woman who had the ability to tempt him like no other woman had ever done before. Tempt him with her blue eyes with whites so white that it looked as though milk had been poured into them, and her serene, lovely smile that hinted of peace in a cruel and crazy world should he dare relinquish his guard and succumb to it. His desire for her was constantly on simmer every time he was in her company. Every time she so much as came into his mind! He was captivated by the graceful yet sexy way she moved, her soft velvet voice made him shiver, and her unerring ability to reduce every vow he made to keep his hands off her to a bare-faced *lie* went without saying.

Gray loved the way she smelled, too—just like a warm summer breeze, even on a cold day when winter bit hard. Just what the *hell* did she think she was doing? Out with Sean Regan, of all people! He swore softly under his breath. He'd known he missed her. But he hadn't realised just how much until he'd seen her there in the flesh with another man. He had a temper, God knew, but he wasn't generally given to violence. For the first time since he had got into scraps at school with the other boys he was genuinely tempted to demonstrate his superior strength to the younger man.

His eyes narrowed as he saw that the two figures on the beach had started walking again. Just what had they been discussing so intently? He'd seen Karen smile—or was it laugh? He resented it like hell that Sean had the ability to make her enjoy herself. He had to clamp down on the almost overwhelming urge to call out—to let her know he was there and demand to know what she was doing out with Sean. And when he got her attention he'd insist that she come home with him to his house, to his bed... Yes, to his bed. Where he'd soon make her forget the younger man's ready smile and easy charm and make her ache and moan and cry out with wanting him instead. *He'd lose himself in her.* He'd drown them both in the scalding heat of their urgent coupling.

An almost painful surge of desire ricocheted through Gray, so that for a moment he forgot to breathe as the world seemed to sway around him.

'What the hell have you done to me, Karen Ford?' He furiously cursed her name out loud, as if to exorcise the effect she was having on him, and Chase pricked up his ears, as if hearing something he longed to hear.

'I know, boy.' Loosening his hold on the thick collar, Gray ruffled the great fawn head. 'You miss her, too, don't you? I'm afraid there's not much I can do about that right now. Not when she's with someone else. Maybe later, though?' An idea stole into his brain. 'Come on. Let's go home.'

Surveying the various outfits she'd laid across the patchwork bedspread, the myriad colours, styles and textures making her bed closely resemble a stall in a Turkish bazaar, Karen sighed. She frowned deeply as she mentally mixed and matched and came up with…nothing too inspiring, to be frank. She'd never been a slave to fashion, nor was it her forte, but she wanted to feel good when she went to see Liz Regan at the newly opened Liz's Cantina.

Should she go for her usual bohemian look? Or would the well-travelled Liz be expecting some trendy upmarket look? She couldn't imagine that that would be the case. The town— although thriving—was situated in a mostly rural area, for goodness' sake. Not in the centre of some busy urban sprawl. It wasn't as if her customers would be young hotshots from the city. Even so, it was still immensely difficult to make up her mind what to wear.

Sighing, she picked out a coral-pink scooped-neck top with narrow pink ribbons threaded through the wrists, and found a long multi-coloured flared skirt that looked vaguely Mexican to match.

Having divested herself of her plain white tee shirt, Karen had the top halfway over her head when there was a knock at the door. She froze. Who in blazes was that? Surely it couldn't be Sean, arriving already? Struggling to tug her top down into place, she angled her wrist to read the time on her watch. Four-fifteen... He was way too early. Oh, well, he'd just have to amuse himself for half an hour while she sorted herself out.

She was still in two minds as to whether she really wanted this job or not. One minute she did—the next she didn't. What did she know about working in a café, for goodness' sake? Not much. But at least she knew how to clean and cook. The little cottage was testimony to that.

Feeling flustered and nervous, she checked her jeans were properly zipped up, then shot out of the bedroom to answer the door, her cheeks burning and her hair tumbling wildly about her shoulders as she went.

'Gray.'

Her heart almost stopped when she saw who her visitor was. Even though she hungrily absorbed his image—like someone nearly drowning who'd just been thrown a lifeline—he transmitted no such similar appreciation or pleasure at seeing her in return.

His grey eyes, naturally cool and aloof at the best of times, looked as if they had frosting on them from the Arctic. The broad shoulders filling her doorway in the customary black leather jacket had fury rolling off them in waves, while his jaw was clenched with barely contained restraint. Restraint that made the arresting planes of his cheekbones seem as though they were carved out of granite. The impression he gave was an austere one, with not so much as a hint of warmth to soften those prickly rough edges. Karen's stomach flipped. What had she done to deserve such a look?

'I've obviously called at a bad time,' he finally said, in a clipped icy tone that warned her his patience was at the end of a very short rope.

'A bad time? Why would you think that? I was just—I was just—'

There was something in the way those disturbing eyes of his dipped suddenly to the region of her chest that made her glance downwards. She saw instantly that her scoop-necked top had not been properly adjusted and totally bared one silky shoulder, where her bra strap had slipped down in her haste to dress. The top of a softly rounded breast was more exposed than it should have been, and that was coupled with her flushed cheeks and disarrayed hair. Karen suddenly realised with devastating horror that her visitor had immediately and *wrongly* put two and two together and made five.

Making a grab for her wayward sleeve, she hiked it up again over her shoulder, and embarrassed heat hotly assailed her as Gray followed every move like the proverbial hawk.

'It's Sean, isn't it?' he ground out.

Because he was so furious Karen automatically stepped back. A violent tremble seized her even as her throat dried up like a desert.

'Wh-what makes you think that?' she stammered.

'Where is he? Is he still here?' Striding angrily into the room, Gray slammed the door shut behind him. He slammed it so hard he almost rocked it right off its hinges.

Sensing herself pale as the discordant sound echoed threateningly round the room, Karen eyed him nervously. 'Gray...' She put out her hand to explain, and found it grabbed and hauled towards him, so that she lost her balance and fell hard against his powerful chest. It was like hitting granite, and for a dangerous moment she was winded and almost overcome by the disturbing scent of fury and heat.

'Was it to get back at me?' he growled into her face, eyes burning hotter than a furnace as they blazed down at her. He was so angry he was scaring her.

'Sean isn't here, Gray.' Her voice rose in protest, and her hands pressed against the warm worn leather of his jacket as she realised his fingers were biting into the soft flesh of her upper arms with scant consideration or care.

'I saw you together on the beach.'

'And you drew your own conclusions?'

Something snapped inside her—because he'd managed to turn a perfectly innocent event into something almost sordid. Who the hell did he think he was, coming into her home and treating her as if she belonged to him in some way? She didn't need his or anybody's permission to do *anything*. She was a totally free agent.

'I can take a walk with whomever I damn well please! You're my landlord, not my keeper.'

Scowling fiercely, Gray abruptly let her go. Then he walked over to the window to stare out at the grassy bank outside, where his mud-splattered Range Rover was parked on the verge. His gaze barely even registered it was there. He was staring beyond it into the distance, where the purple shaded mountains loomed darkly to the right and the sea to the left. Inside, his heart was beating way too fast. He'd never experienced jealousy like this. *Never!* Maura would attest to that. Hell, any number of women in his past could attest to that. That had been one of their most persistent gripes. Gray hadn't cared enough for any of them to be jealous. *Until now...*

Turning slowly back into the room, he boldly regarded the reason for his painful introspection. In the revealing pink top, her creamy breasts pressed unknowingly provocatively against the flimsy fabric. Her long golden hair was sexily mussed, and her blue eyes clear as polished crystal. Karen was surely the epitome of male fantasy. Raw aching need slammed into him like a train hurtling at full speed into a wall as he drank in the vision of her. He told himself that it didn't matter that Sean Regan had bedded her first. It hurt like hell, but he'd get over it. Gray still wanted her.

'If you're suggesting that something went on between Sean and me,' Karen began, her hands nervously clasped together in front of her waist, 'absolutely nothing did. We went for a walk—that's all.'

'Why?' There was a sudden lessening of the tight band of tension round his chest. He wanted to believe her. Right now Gray wanted it more than anything else in the whole wide world. Wanted it more than he wanted to paint—and that was the supreme accolade as far as he was concerned, because painting was his *life*.

'Why?' That endearing little way she had of frowning lightly crumpled her brow, and Gray's mouth went dry. Even the way she frowned was sexy. 'Because he asked me to.' She shrugged, as if it should be obvious.

'What did he want?'

'Look…I don't understand why all these questions. I've done nothing wrong. I don't see that I have to answer to you anyway. Up until a few weeks ago I didn't even know you existed.'

'Well, you know now.' Pushing himself away from the window where he'd been leaning, Gray started to move slowly towards her. He emitted the same raw energy as an athlete at the peak of his fitness, and the air all but crackled round him. Karen's focus involuntarily slid from his enigmatic laserlike gaze to the long, muscular legs encased in fitted black jeans. It didn't take a professor of human biology to deduce that he was more than a little aroused, and she forced herself to inhale a shaky, steadying breath, because suddenly she knew she was way out of her depth—*drowning* in fact.

'So you weren't in bed with Sean when I knocked?' The sexy timbre of his voice all but pinned her to the floor.

'As if I— Search the bedroom if you want!' She bit her lip to stop herself from crying. This was absurd. Did he really believe she was so desperate for physical contact that she'd jump into bed with the next man who asked her? *As if her desire for Gray could be so easily transferred*—as if it was a mere whim instead of a soul-destroying, earth-shattering experience that kept her awake at nights, aching and longing for just the mere sight of him? Nothing made sense any more because of him. She should be grieving for her husband, not pining after some cold, cynical stranger who was too angry and wounded to be kind.

'I don't need to do that. I'll take your word for it.' Sighing heavily, he drew his hand round the back of his neck, as if he'd been under strain. But then, incredibly, the corners of his mouth curved in a near dazzling smile that came totally out of the blue, and Karen's insides were submerged in the sensual warmth of heated honey.

She caught her breath, inwardly struggling to appear calm. Why should he have things all his own way? Just because he hit her where it hurt with that unfair killer smile, it didn't mean that she had to turn to putty in his hands. Even though she knew she easily could. His presence alone had the power to make her feel exhilarated and alive. More exhilarated and alive than she'd ever felt before. But she knew that he could also make her plunge to the depths of misery, and she wouldn't forgive him for his Neanderthal behaviour that quickly. Yet again he'd hurt her with his thoughtless innuendoes and she had every right to be furious.

'Am I supposed to be grateful?'

'Never mind that—are you planning on taking more walks with Sean any time soon?'

'That's none of your business.'

'I'm making it my business.'

The smile went as quickly as it had appeared, leaving in its place a dark, brooding intensity that made Karen regret her tart reply. Should she tell him that Sean was expected at any time now? That his sister wanted to see her about a potential job? Why put herself in the firing line again? she thought. It would keep. She'd done nothing wrong, and refused to be made to feel as though she had.

'I can't accept that when it's totally unreasonable. Anyway...' She glanced meaningfully down at her watch. Four-thirty... Sean would be here in fifteen minutes. She had to get her skates on if she was going to be ready, and regrettably she had to get Gray to leave—or she'd be a nervous wreck by the time the younger man arrived. 'I'm going out very shortly. Thanks for dropping by.' She lowered her gaze because his brooding hot glance was scorching her. 'Even if it was only to tear me off a strip.'

'Where are you off to?'

She'd been praying he wouldn't ask her that, and now all the blood rushed dizzyingly to her head. Telling him that she was off out with Sean—albeit on a perfectly innocent expedition—would surely be tantamount to rubbing salt into an already open wound. But all the same she was going to have to tell him the truth, because she couldn't lie. Not outright.

'I'm going to see someone about a job.' She crossed her arms in front of her, still conscious of the fact that the pink top wasn't perhaps the most suitable item of clothing she could have chosen to wear. Gray had hardly taken his eyes off her figure since he'd come in—a fact that was making her more than a little hot under the collar.

'I didn't know you were looking for work.' He frowned, as if the thought disturbed him.

'I wasn't.' Karen shrugged. 'But someone thought I might be interested in this particular job.'

'So what is it?'

She moistened her lips with her tongue. The interest this innocent action evoked in the tall, rugged man standing just bare inches away from her was instant and tangible. It emanated from him like an electrical current that hit her squarely, deeply in the solar plexus. Swallowing hard, she felt her nipples suddenly surge against the thin barricade of her top, her stomach muscles tighten uncomfortably. Shifting onto her opposite hip, she lifted her chin to help bolster her confidence. 'I don't know, exactly. That's what I'm hopefully going to find out.'

'Are you telling me you need the work?'

'I wasn't aware that I was telling you anything very much at all. And stop quizzing me...I don't like it.' Exasperated by his questioning, which somehow managed to make her feel ridiculously guilty even though she hadn't done anything to warrant it, Karen moved across to the bedroom door, anxious that she wouldn't be ready by the time Sean appeared. Somehow she had to get Gray to leave before that.

'Karen? Are you short of money? I can help you out if you are.' His statement was so surprising that it stopped her in her tracks, and she turned to study him, blue eyes widening in bemusement.

'No...I'm not. I wasn't considering the job for that reason. I don't mean that as it sounds—I'm not a millionaire by any stretch—but I'm okay financially for now. Thanks all the same.'

She was very fortunate that Ryan had left her comfortable in that department, and her own earnings had made a sizeable contribution. Still, she was somewhat taken aback by the idea that Gray would willingly help her out, as he'd so succinctly put it. Again he'd surprised her. Like turning up with the new furniture and giving the sitting room a fresh coat of paint himself, when surely a man of his purported wealth could easily afford to pay someone to take care of such mundane tasks for him? It was difficult to equate his willingness to offer help with the often abrasive arrogance of the man.

'I really have to get ready now.'

'I can give you a lift if you're going into town? I can even wait and bring you back…'

The leather sleeve of his jacket squeaked a little roughly as he raised his hand to wipe perspiration from his brow. The movement dislodged the wayward black lock of hair that usually dropped back onto his forehead, and Karen saw the double row of faint yet distinct lines indented in his slightly weather-beaten skin. There was something that touched her deeply about the sight—as if those lines had been put there by too much suffering—and she knew a sorely intense need to offer him some kind of comfort. But now wasn't exactly the right moment. Not when time and commitment were constraining her.

'Sean's coming to collect me. He's taking me and bringing me back as far as I know.' She let her hand drop helplessly to her side instead of pushing wide the door to the bedroom, where she'd been about to go and change, witnessing the sudden flash of angry emotion in Gray's clenched jaw and narrowed glare with trepidation.

'I see.'

'No, you *don't* see!' Karen burst out, exasperated. 'It's his sister Liz who wants to see me about the job. She's opened up a café and is looking for help. Sean told her about my baking and gave her some of my fruitcake to try. She thought I might be interested in working for her.'

When this explanation failed to elicit any response from

Gray, verbal or otherwise—nothing but a darkly smouldering glare, in fact—she threw up her hands and groaned.

'She sent Sean to ask me about it. He's only collecting me as a favour to his sister. It's hardly a big deal, is it?'

'That rather depends on whether Sean thinks it is or not.'

CHAPTER SIX

'WHAT do you mean?' Karen's expression was as guileless as a newborn babe's, and Gray was torn between the need either to shake her or pull her into his arms and stop her talking altogether with a long, drugging kiss. The woman had been married for five years, for God's sake, yet she acted like a total innocent when it came to men. He shook his head slowly from side to side, trying to figure it out.

'Do I really have to spell it out for you? You're a beautiful girl. Sean's a young, unattached, *reasonably* good-looking male. Am I making it any clearer?'

The penny dropped. Anxiously, Karen drove her fingers through her hair. 'He doesn't see me that way.' She willed away the faint, nagging thought that perhaps he did, and like Scarlet O'Hara resolved to deal with it tomorrow. 'Besides, I'm not in the market for any kind of romantic liaison.'

'That a fact?'

'You don't have to act like you know everything. Especially when you clearly don't.'

The sound of a vehicle pulling up outside had them both turning their heads towards the window. 'I've got to finish getting ready,' Karen muttered, deliberately avoiding Gray's disturbing glance.

'He makes so much as one move on you and I'll knock his

block off,' he asserted irritably, fists bunching down by his sides.

'How charming… And that's how you treat a friend, is it?'

Gray scowled. 'He's not a friend, just someone who occasionally works for me. I don't have any friends. Nor do I need any.'

Shaking her head in dismay, Karen started to head through the open bedroom door. 'I don't have time for this.'

'Just so you know—I'll be back later this evening.'

'Why? What on earth for?' She glanced back at him over her shoulder.

'Now, there's a leading question if ever I heard one.' Grinning like the devil himself, he opened the front door and strode outside.

Sean was just getting out of his van when Gray reached him. 'Hello, Gray.' The younger man gave him an uneasy smile. As he straightened, his occasional employer frowned warningly.

'If you're thinking of asking her out on a date…*don't*,' he growled. 'She's come here to heal—to get over the death of her husband.'

'She's a widow?'

'Be respectful, and don't—*don't*—go looking for anything you shouldn't.' The frown that was already etched on Gray's handsome face intensified.

'Sure, I'm only taking her to see my sister about a job,' Sean replied defensively.

'That's all well and good. Just make sure you bring her straight home afterwards.'

'I really don't think that—'

'It's any of my business?' Gray interrupted with a wolfish glare. 'Well, that's where you're wrong. As far as— Never mind!'

Clearly deciding he'd said enough, the older man strode away with his usual impatient stride, and Sean heard the Range Rover's engine fire up behind him.

Liz Regan, Sean's sister, was pretty as a pixie, with cropped red hair, merry green eyes and a slender, tiny frame, and Karen liked her on sight. She also liked what she'd done in turning a once dilapidated old building into a trendy but friendly Mexican café, with terracotta-tiled floors, pumpkin-yellow and blue walls, and sturdy wooden furniture. The tables had yellow vinyl cloths with pictures of fruit depicted on them. As the last two customers of the day paid their bills and left, Liz whipped off the sunny yellow apron she'd been wearing over her tee shirt and jeans, grabbed Karen's hand and led her into the back room she clearly used as an office.

'You look like just the kind of shot in the arm this place could benefit from,' she declared, grinning, furnishing her brother Sean, who was lounging in the doorway, with a wink at the same time. 'And you smell as good as you look, too. I won't be able to keep those frisky lads away if you come to work for me, Karen.'

'Sean said that you needed some help… What kind of thing were you thinking of, exactly?'

'I've heard you're great at baking the cakes. Being the proprietor and all, I don't always have time to do much my-self—even though I love it. There's a local woman that works part-time doing a good bit of the baking right now, but I could really use another hand. Think you'd be interested?'

'Well, I—'

'It wouldn't be just the baking,' the other woman said hurriedly. 'Having seen you, I think I'd really like you somewhere visible—front of house, so to speak. You're so pretty you'd bring in the male population in their droves!'

Bemused, Karen shrugged. 'I've never been a waitress before…but I suppose I could learn.'

Glancing at Sean, Liz grinned. 'What else can you do? What are your strengths?' Liz drew out the well-worn chair with a curved backrest that sat in front of her desk, then with a nod of her head indicated that Karen sit down.

Linking her hands as she made herself comfortable, in her mind her nervous visitor scanned the meagre list of things she considered she was good at.

'My strengths are that I'm a quick learner, and I'll do a good job whatever I have to do. But I suppose more than anything I can confidently say that I can clean and cook… I've never tried cooking Mexican before, but I'm willing to be your assistant if that would be of use?'

'A general assistant with paperwork and managing the place, maybe, but I've already got someone who does the Mexican cooking. So is there anything else you can do?'

'Like what, for instance?'

Under her ribs, Karen's heart had started to knock. She was slightly deflated that cleaning and cooking and being an assistant might not be good enough for this diminutive, colourful woman to employ her—not that she'd exactly pinned her hopes on getting a job here in the first place—and old feelings of insecurity couldn't help but surface.

'Do you have great ideas? Are you good with people? Can you sing? That kind of thing.'

Now Karen's heart started to thump even louder. Across the room, as if sensing her discomfort, Sean threw her a reassuring smile.

'Can I sing?'

'Sure—everybody likes a tune here. I was thinking some kind of entertainment in the lunch hour a couple of times a week while folks eat their meal would be a great selling point.'

Did this place get enough customers to warrant entertainment in the lunch hour? Karen wondered in further bemusement. Meeting Liz Regan's dancing emerald eyes, she suddenly knew that if anyone could make such a maverick venture a success it was *her*. Clearing her throat, she smoothed some drifting strands of hair away from the side of her face and sat up straighter.

'Yes, I can sing.'

'You can? I don't suppose you play an instrument as well?'

Karen smiled. Inside her chest, her heartbeat resumed its normal beat at last. Now she was confident that this was something she *did* excel at. 'Guitar,' she replied. 'I play the acoustic guitar.'

'Eureka!'

To Karen's surprise, Liz hauled her out of the chair and danced round the room with her.

'Liz…for God's sake, what are you doing?' Sean grabbed his sister's arm to curb her enthusiasm, but she still whirled round and round with a helplessly laughing Karen.

When she came to a sudden standstill, Karen pushed the hair from her eyes breathing hard. 'You don't even know if I can really sing a note!' she exclaimed.

'Can you?' The grin plastered across the other girl's wide mouth froze, as though the possibility had never even crossed her mind.

'I sang professionally,' Karen admitted, her heartbeat racing slightly again. It was perhaps only at that moment that she realised how terribly she'd missed the pleasure of performing—'singing for her supper', as Ryan had used to teasingly call it—and how much she longed to do it again.

'You did?' Now it was Sean's turn to look surprised.

'I did. My late husband was my manager.'

'You're a widow?' Liz's expression turned serious.

'I am. But moving here has been really good for me…
helping me come to terms, if you know what I mean?'

'I knew you were special the moment I first clapped eyes
on you. There's a light round you that draws the gaze. And
it's not just because you're the prettiest thing this town has
seen in years, Karen Ford!'

Spearing icy fingers through his rain-dampened black hair
as he stood outside Karen's door that evening, all thought
of discomfort and cold left Gray as the music drifting out
from the house made him still. She must be playing the radio.
Whatever the song was that accompanied the gently strumming guitar he heard, it was riveting…*haunting*. The singer
had a rare talent.

Before he knew it the backs of his eyes were pricking with
tears. He rarely ever listened to music these days, but his father
Paddy had loved it with a passion. He'd often been found at
Malloy's Bar on a Saturday night, tapping his feet to whatever
tunes were on offer, for a while forgetting his troubles and
helping to numb them with a pint of Guinness, or three…

Grimacing, Gray raised his fist and pounded on the door.
Instantly the music inside stopped. The urgency which submerged his senses every time he thought of Karen gripped him
with a vengeance as he silently asserted that her enjoyment of
the music on the radio would have to be postponed until he'd
had his fill of her company this evening. He'd spent a miserable afternoon imagining her with Sean, and the antique clock
on the mantelpiece had barely chimed seven o'clock before
he was striding from the house and climbing into his car to
make his way here. *To make his way to her…*

Gray's heart thudded hard when she opened the door.

'Oh…it's you.'

He hated it that she seemed disappointed to see him. Was it
Sean she'd been hoping would knock on her door this evening?

Jealousy stabbed through his insides with all the stinging hurt of a hot dagger. Wearing black leggings, a black silk top and a red fringed cotton scarf draped round her shoulders, with her pretty hair left long and loose and her blue eyes shooting irritated sparks at him, right then Karen was the answer to any prayer for good fortune to visit him that Gray had ever prayed.

'Yes, it's me. I said I'd drop by, remember?'

'You'd better come in, then, I suppose.'

She held the door wide, albeit reluctantly. Swallowing down his regret that she wasn't happier to see him, he went inside. The first thing that he registered on entering the small sitting room, after the soporific perfume of scented candles, was the acoustic guitar propped up against the couch. His brow puckered, then his stomach clenched.

'I heard music just now, while I was waiting outside the door…I thought it was the radio.' Gray hadn't meant for the remark to sound accusing, but somehow it did, and he found himself silently cursing the lack of sensitivity that seemed to be ever growing the more time he spent on his own.

'I suppose you're going to tell me now that it's not allowed for a tenant to play the guitar?'

'Don't be foolish.' He jammed his cold hands into the pockets of his leather jacket. He was tempted to cross to the fire crackling in the grate to warm them, but he wouldn't concede to any such comfort until he'd reassured the woman in front of him that he hadn't come to visit her merely to be difficult. His glance cleaved to her as though magnetised, and he knew it didn't hide the hunger building inside him. 'Was that you singing?'

Folding her arms across her chest, Karen sucked in a breath. 'Yes…it was me.'

Gray dropped his voice in awe. 'The sound almost stopped my heart.'

She flushed, then stared down at the ground.

Seeing how the compliment undid her, he closed the gap between them. Without giving himself time to change his mind, he impelled her urgently into his arms. 'You're a surprise and a delight, *a mhuirnín*...'

'Your hands are freezing.'

'That may be so, but inside I'm burning up...burning up from wanting you so bad that I can't think of anything else.' His voice a husky grate, Gray cupped her face, stroking her soft satin cheeks with the sides of his thumbs.

She trembled, her warm breath drifting over him like a scented summer breeze. 'We wouldn't be good for each other Gray.'

Her voice had a catch in it, but even before she'd finished speaking he was kissing her, plundering her mouth as if she was supplying life-giving oxygen. He hardly knew his own name any more. He'd yearned to hold her...to *love* her if she'd let him...

'How do you know until we try?' he whispered.

Flattening her palms against his chest, Karen tried vainly to push him away.

'I may have gone a little crazy lately, but I'm not some witless lemming about to hurl myself over the edge of a cliff—because that's what I'd be doing if I let you—if I let you—' She broke off to bite her lip, and Gray saw that her beautiful sky-blue eyes had grown moist.

'If you let me what? Keep the cold away for a little while?'

As if surrendering the urge to somehow try and stem the powerful attraction that flowed between them Karen laid her head against him. Holding her to him with a sigh, Gray stroked his palm over her hair, murmuring soft words in Irish as he marvelled at its silken fall as well as silently registering the warm quivering curves of her compact slender body. 'Hush,

hush, *a chailín álainn*.' He'd never felt as protective or possessive of a woman before. Briefly closing his eyes, he kissed
the top of her head.

Lifting her gaze, Karen stared up at him. 'If I let you keep
out the cold for a little while? That's all it will be?'

'If that's all that you want.'

'You won't expect anything more from what we share?'

Fielding the jolt of dismay that hurt his heart, Gray stoically
bit back his disappointment. 'No.'

'Then neither will I.' Curling her palm inside his, Karen
glanced wistfully back into his eyes as she led him into her
bedroom in silence.

When she saw he was going to reach for her first, to help her
undress, Karen gripped the front of Gray's still damp leather
jacket as though indicating no, and then slowly, carefully,
slipped it from his shoulders. His quixotic grey eyes were
full of longing, and she sensed the powerful self-restraint
he had to employ to keep from hauling her roughly to him.
A dizzying, almost *painful* excitement gathered force inside
her, making her shiver. Gray O'Connell was a man hardened
and embittered by his past, but with his wind-tossed raven
hair and feral, hungry gaze he was heartbreakingly beautiful
as well as wounded, and right then he was everything she
needed…even if ultimately the fire he stoked in her would
burn her to cinders.

'For pity's sake, Karen!' He was all but shaking as she continued to methodically remove his sweater, then the maroon
tee shirt he wore underneath. Both were cast heedlessly onto
the floor.

The faint, musky warmth of his body sent a wave of aching
desire bolting through her blood that threatened to buckle
her already shaking knees. Gazing in nervous wonder at the
display of strongly toned muscle beneath the fine little coils

of ebony hair on his chest, she couldn't resist laying her open palm there, softly stroking it across the flat male nipples and feeling him tense with longing beneath her touch. Lifting her glance, Karen silently registered the near desperation she saw in his gaze and slid her hand over his sculpted high cheekbone to push her fingers curiously through his unruly mane of dark hair. *It was far softer than it looked.* Just like raw silk.

'Do you want to drive me insane? Do you?' With a growl, Gray grabbed hold of her hand and pressed a hot kiss deep into the centre of her palm.

'You're beautiful,' she said softly. 'I just wanted to see you.'

'And I want to see you in all your glory, too. But more than that I need you in my arms, before I die from the sheer agony of wanting you.'

After hastily removing his jeans, Karen was at last hauled against him and lifted high against his chest as Gray eagerly carried her to the bed. She had already turned down the sheets in preparation for her night's rest, and the smooth cotton was cool against her heated skin, even through her clothes. But Gray soon removed the last flimsy barriers between them to sit astride her, his strong thigh muscles trapping her between them before lowering his dark head to steal a deeply voracious kiss.

It was a kiss such as she had never experienced before—a kiss that flooded her with such intoxicating heat that she barely registered the soft moans that filled the air as her own. The wild ocean-swept taste of his mouth and tongue stoked her longing to a level almost beyond bearing. When his lips closed over one burgeoning tight nipple, his teeth grazing the tender flesh there, Karen gasped her shock and desire. *When Ryan had been intimate with her it had never been like this... had never created this wild storm of need that ripped her from her moorings and threatened to cast her out to sea for ever...*

She wanted to weep at what felt like the worst betrayal of the love she had shared with her husband. But she remembered, too, that he'd often been uncomfortable with the desire she'd sometimes expressed for more uninhibited intimacy, telling her that it was a fact of life that some men had a lower sex drive than others and he was sorry but that was just the way it was for him. He might not be able to love her in the way she needed, but he promised he would put every ounce of his effort into helping her forge a wonderful career and being the best, most devoted friend she could ever have...

Karen shut out the unwanted recollection as she lost herself in Gray's ardent drugging kiss. Her hands slid down his long muscled back to cup his taut firm buttocks, and his expression of pleasure was instant and vocal. That unrestrained, almost *feral* sound made her feel more desirable and womanly than she'd ever felt before. Silently she acknowledged she *wanted* to be ripped from the moorings that anchored her too painfully to the past—she *wanted* to be somehow set free. Free to fall or fly—she didn't care which right then...

'I want...'

'What do you want, my beautiful little songbird, hmm?'

Her lover kissed the side of her neck just behind her ear, making Karen quiver. Her hips grew soft and pliant as volcanic heat flooded into her centre.

'More of this?' Gray teased as he palmed her breasts and then pinched her nipples until she almost came up off the bed.

'Yes!' she rasped, almost delirious with need.

Raising his head, then sitting up, Gray reached for the jeans he had thrown onto the bed before taking Karen into his arms and hurriedly sheathing his hardened sex with the protection he'd brought.

Transfixed by the honed male beauty of his strongly corded arms and chest, shyly observing how well endowed he was, Karen didn't waste time speculating on the fact that he'd been so sure of her capitulation he'd come prepared. *What would be the point?* They were both adults—both knew that the near *violent* chemistry they shared would sooner or later have to have an outlet.

But she was shivering so hard that it was almost impossible to relax. Clearly some fear and tension had inadvertently crept into her reckless bid for sensual freedom. Might it even be *guilt?* In any case it was a long time since she had been with a man, so when Gray started to penetrate her, even as her mouth hungrily melded with his and their tongues hotly entwined, she couldn't help the little gasp of pain that left her.

'What's wrong? Am I hurting you?' He stared down at her in the dusk-filled room, surprising her with the genuine concern that she saw blazing from his long-lashed eyes.

'No. I'm fine. There's nothing wrong.' *She didn't want his kindness.* If he was kind to her then that might make her care for him too much. That was a risk she didn't want to entertain for long. Wanting Gray O'Connell to stay in her life would be like trying to hold on to a sea breeze, or to the morning birdsong that died away when winter came. 'Just hold me,' she murmured.

'I'll do more than that, *a stór*... I'm going to take you to a place where we can both be free for a time...free from grief and pain...that's a promise.'

Another gasp left her as he penetrated her fully and then, like a big cat, watched her register her pleasure and surprise, a small knowing smile playing about his roguish lips. Gray's loving of her body was hard, strong and demanding, and Karen revelled in it with every fibre of her being as she had never revelled in this most intimate act before, meeting every thrust with a lift of her hips to take him even deeper inside her.

So lost was she in the sensual ride that she couldn't say when it changed to an unstoppable rocket, taking her to the stars, but she heard Gray's deeply gravelled tone urging her onwards. Tears washed into her eyes as she flew apart in his arms.

As revelations went, it was pretty damned wonderful. That was why she cried. And it had happened so quickly and so easily. She hadn't even had to try. It grieved her to admit it, but with Ryan that part of their lovemaking had always been a cause of great frustration for Karen. Knowing that her husband could more or less live without sex had seemed to inhibit her ability to just let go and enjoy the act when they *did* spend time in bed together.

But now, even as the warm salty trail of tears slid into her mouth, a savage cry from Gray near shook the rafters as he held himself still inside her for long seconds and then shuddered hard. Catching his stunned glance as the waves of sensual fulfilment washing through her began slowly to ebb, Karen reached up and drew his head down between her breasts. His warm breath, unshaven jaw and the heavy weight of his strong, fit body pressing her down into the mattress felt like the nearest thing to heaven she could imagine…

CHAPTER SEVEN

THE intoxicating scent of Karen's body aroused an inexplicable longing in Gray for something he couldn't or wouldn't name as she tenderly cradled his head between her breasts. The realisation unsettled him, made him quickly bring his attention back to the physical aspect of their union...something he definitely *could* handle. His climax had sent his pleasure thermometer shooting right off the scale into another stratosphere, but it hadn't quelled his insurmountable need for her. Again he sensed himself harden.

Reaching out for the tissue box beside the bed, he disposed of the latex protection he'd sheathed himself with and, keeping his passionate gaze locked with Karen's, fitted a fresh one. Desire was swift as a flaming arrow, shooting through him as he began once again to move inside her. Rising up so that he could observe her, he smiled, enjoying the expression of surprise and languorous pleasure on her face. In the fading dusk her blue eyes were dark sapphire, with the emphasis on *fire*, and her beautiful mouth was a lush, sensual paradise he could easily explore for the rest of his life...

Silently, she lifted her hands to cup his face and pull him down to her, gifting him with a hot, sexy kiss. Near on fire with lust, Gray altered his position, urging Karen on top of him. Even before she settled her delicious peachlike rear across his arrow-straight hips he was pushing inside her, desperate to maintain the seismic contact that he knew awaited him. He groaned as she started to rock her hips, not just taking delight in the time-honoured motion of passionate lovers everywhere but in the sight of her gorgeous face, her tumbling honey-gold hair and ravishing pert breasts. He promised himself he would paint her, vowing the study would be his best work yet...

'You're a goddess—but even that description doesn't do your loveliness justice.'

When Karen opened her mouth to reply, Gray's hands enfolded her hips to pull her down even more firmly onto his silken rigid shaft and hold her there. Her dazzling blue eyes widened and ragged breath punched from her lungs. For long seconds he was deluged with the most incredible sensations of unbelievable connection, as well as a fierce longing for a way to make this breathless pleasure last for ever.

But in amongst that longing doubt reared its head. *He didn't deserve her*, he reflected painfully. *But, by God, now that he had her he wouldn't let her go in a hurry!* Making love with Karen was everything Gray had dreamt it would be, and no stain or recrimination from his past or guilt about her husband dying would keep him from hoping for more...

Karen woke in the early hours of the morning to the rapid tattoo of rain against the window. But as she adjusted the eiderdown more snugly across a chilly bare shoulder she examined the still sleeping man lying by her side. In the depths of slumber the two faint furrows crossing his brow were relaxed, barely discernible, and the sensual mouth was free of cynicism and hurt, innocent as a child's.

Gray's regret over his father not accepting his decision to forge his own way in life and his sad, ignominious death on a lonely beach clearly tormented Gray—tormented and *punished* him—as did the terrible fact of his mother's suicide.

Empathising with his sadness, Karen sighed, gently touching his bristly beard-shadowed jawline with her fingertips.

After returning home from her interview with Liz, she'd tried hard not to keep anticipating his promised visit that evening. After all, he could so easily change his mind. He was still an unknown entity to her...an unpredictable maverick. But even as she'd sat singing and strumming her guitar, trying to recall songs that had at one time been second nature to her—songs that she might perhaps perform at the café—her insides had swooped and dived every time the image of Gray's hauntingly handsome face had stolen into her mind.

Now his muscular arm was anchored possessively round her waist. Whenever she moved even slightly it immediately tightened again, as if he was determined not to let her go—even in sleep.

Reflecting on the passion they'd shared over and over again, before succumbing to an exhausted slumber, Karen felt her heart leap with hope that something good might ensue from their liaison, and prayed that it wouldn't end badly as she secretly feared it might. Gray had unlocked something deep inside her that her loving husband had never been able to release. For the first time in twenty-six years she felt womanly, desired and confident of her femininity, and as she lay there beside him she sensed a new resolve building inside her. A resolve that she wouldn't be frightened to try new things any more—that she would embrace life. She would allow herself to experience enjoyment whether she believed she deserved it or not. Most of all she would stop searching for approval all the time—and that included her mother's...

Burrowing her head between Gray's arm and hard-muscled shoulder, she spread her palm out across the dark swirl of soft hair on his chest—and drifted back off to sleep.

When she woke again, sounds emanated from the kitchen that definitely suggested tea being made. Sniffing the air, she also scented toast. Briefly stretching her lips in a smile, she plumped up the pillows behind her, then sat up. Grabbing the edge of the pretty patchwork eiderdown to cover her naked breasts, she was just in time to ensure her modesty—because, seconds later, the bedroom door was flung wide to admit the arresting reason for the sounds in the kitchen. His dark hair uncombed and tousled from sleep, his jeans riding low across his hips and his chest and feet tantalisingly bare, Gray was bearing a tray with two mugs—one tea, one coffee—and a plate of hot buttered toast. In all her days Karen had never seen a sexier or more welcome sight.

'Good morning.' Her insides clenched tight as she strove to subdue the intense carnal ache that automatically throbbed through her.

'Morning,' he replied, his voice a little husky. 'I've made breakfast.'

'So I see.'

'You're not surprised, then, at the extent of my talents?'

Karen blushed at the innuendo in his voice and the lingering sexy glance he gave her. 'I'm not surprised at all,' she murmured, tugging the eiderdown up a little higher over her breasts.

'What are you doing?' Leaving the tray on the small cabinet beside the bed, Gray suddenly gave her his undivided attention.

'What do you mean?'

'Why are you covering yourself up?'

Karen didn't know what to say. The temperature in the room was comfortably warm, despite the hammering rain outside—how could it not be after the heat they'd radiated last night?—so she could hardly use being cold as an excuse for pulling up the eiderdown.

'I—'

She held on to the material with a near death-grip, but her

fingers were prised gently but firmly away as Gray tugged the bedspread free, letting it fold gently round her waist. She shivered as the kiss of air stroked its feathery fingers across her naked skin—but again *not* because she was cold. There was little chance of being cold with her lover's fire-lit glance blazing hungrily back at her.

Dropping down onto the bed beside her, he made no pretence of looking anywhere else but at her bared breasts, the dusky nipples already puckering tightly beneath his bold examination.

'If Shakespeare himself had witnessed you as I do now he would have composed a sonnet to these beautiful breasts.' He smiled. 'And Byron would have surpassed himself with an incandescent poem in your honour.'

Just as she reached forward to grab the eiderdown Gray dipped his head to capture a tingling sensitive nipple between his lips. His even white teeth clamped down a little on the already raised flesh, and the bolt of pleasure-pain that flashed through her made Karen helplessly yelp as he started to suckle hard.

'Oh, my God!'

He glanced up at her, the look in his long-lashed eyes lascivious and unrepentant. 'Is that "Oh, my God, I don't want this?" or "Oh, my God, this is so good I don't want you to stop?"' he challenged huskily.

'What do you think?' Karen answered low-voiced, and she settled her palms either side of his unshaven jaw, then drove her fingers a little desperately through his hair...

Liz had said she wanted to try an entertainment slot two lunchtimes a week to start with, and Karen was relieved that she didn't expect more. Although she'd been practising as much as she could, she somehow felt she was a complete rookie, starting up again like this. Since Ryan's death she had barely sung a note.

There was also another reason for maybe not giving her rehearsals her utmost concentration. Her evenings had become snared by another more compelling distraction…*Gray*. He'd taken to calling in on her around the time of her evening meal. Sometimes he ate with her. Other times, when his mood was dark and he didn't want to engage in even the smallest pleasantries, he took her by the hand and led her straight into the bedroom.

If he was using their passionate lovemaking to help stave off some of the demons that haunted him, Karen told herself she didn't mind—so long as he found some peace for a while. *It shocked her to realise how much she was putting his wellbeing before her own, and how dangerous that was, but somehow she couldn't seem to help herself.* The man had seriously got into her blood. Sometimes he fell asleep in her arms, but often he woke in the early hours and went home. He usually used Chase as his excuse for leaving. The hound missed him when he wasn't around, he told her, and Bridie his housekeeper—capable as she was—couldn't handle him as he could.

Now, standing in a clear space in Liz's Cantina one busy lunchtime, with the seriously appetising smell of Mexican cooking wafting out from the kitchen, Karen watched the ever-obliging Sean plug in the small amplifier he'd found for her to use and attach her guitar lead. Several patrons turned their heads expectantly towards her as they ate their meals or waited for their food to arrive. Liz had informed her earlier that she and Sean had 'put the word out' about Karen singing, and that was why they were busier than usual. Nervously, she began to tune her guitar. The amplified sound was deep and rich, and she mentally revised the small programme of songs she'd chosen.

Last night she'd told Gray she was performing today, and she'd secretly hoped he would show up to support her, even though he'd shrugged and said, 'I don't doubt you'll be great, sweetheart,' then slid his gaze cagily away without commenting further. Scanning the collection of heads again, already guessing he probably wouldn't show, she bit back her disappointment and made herself smile.

Sean had also set up a microphone, and now he stepped up beside her to give her shoulder a reassuring squeeze. 'Best of luck,' he said in her ear. 'Not that you'll need it.'

Karen wanted to tell him that he and his sister had misplaced their trust in her…that she really wasn't very good. *They hadn't even insisted she audition, for goodness' sake!* But then she remembered the resolution she'd made that first time she and Gray had made love. That she would no longer compulsively seek approval—that she would have much more faith in herself.

'Hi,' she said into the microphone with a smile. People smiled back, and a young lad with dyed black hair and ripped jeans sitting at a table by the door with another youth similarly attired wolf-whistled. 'My name's Karen Ford, and I've been asked to do a few numbers for you. This first one is called "From the Heart."'

From the moment she strummed the opening chord it was as though something so familiar and natural in her took over that barely any effort at all was required. Everything just came together perfectly on its own. The audience was almost deathly quiet as she sang, but as soon as the number came to an end they were applauding hard and calling out for more. Standing by the ranch-style doors to the kitchen, Liz Regan, in her swirling Mexican-style skirt and indigo tee shirt, was perhaps clapping the hardest of all. She even gave several piercing whistles. Meeting the other girl's eyes across the room, Karen guessed she had made a friend in the avant-garde Irishwoman—an ally as well, perhaps?

Flushed with pleasure that her music had gone down so well, she got ready to perform the next number with much more confidence.

Then Gray walked in and she froze.

It was raining again, and the broad shoulders of his battered leather jacket gleamed with damp, almost steaming in the heat of the warm café. His mercurial, almost *fevered* gaze fell on her straight away.

There was no doubt his presence had caused a minor shockwave. Even as Karen's own heartbeat registered his appearance with a jolt, she made herself turn to Sean and ask him for a chair. Suddenly her legs felt like damp noodles, and if she didn't sit down soon they might just crumple beneath her. As she announced the next number she saw Liz fly across the room to guide Gray to a nearby empty table, just as if he was some sort of VIP. A chair was pulled out for him, and Liz must have asked him if he'd like anything to drink. Karen saw him mouth the word 'later.' Then he planted his elbows on the cheerful yellow vinyl tablecloth and gave his utmost attention to Karen.

To Gray's surprise, last night Karen had confessed to him that she'd sung professionally and had been about to sign a record deal when her husband had suddenly died. The deal had never been signed. Instead she'd retreated from the world of music, and when that hadn't seemed to help—her words— she'd escaped to Ireland. He'd heard what she was capable of with his own ears that evening outside her door, but now it hit Gray afresh what a sublime talent she was.

Sensing the tangible ripple of excitement circulating the room, he noticed that people were listening to Karen sing rather than eating their meals. But, more than that, the sight of her sitting there alone with her guitar damn near stopped his heart. She was dressed in well-worn but neatly pressed denims, and a multi-coloured knitted cardigan over a plain white tee shirt, her pretty hair unbound and catching the one thin ray of sunlight that broke through the rainclouds to highlight the honey-gold strands. His stomach knotted with tension and need. He'd spent hours last night with her body pressed up close to his, but it hadn't subdued the powerful desire in him to have her close all the time, to keep her to himself... Yet the moment she started to sing and strum her guitar Gray knew it would be wrong to try and monopolise her attention exclusively.

A talent and a loving personality like Karen's should be shared equally, he realised with a painful stab in the region of his heart. Maybe he should leave her alone?

Even as the thought came to him Gray irritably snuffed it out like a guttering candle. He wished he was stronger, but he couldn't deny himself the one thing that made him feel halfway human again...

After waiting until Karen's song came to an end he beckoned to the ever watchful and attentive Liz Regan to order a double shot of whiskey...

Going into the kitchen to fill the kettle, Karen sensed Gray follow her. His brooding presence was making the tight knot of anxiety beneath her ribs tighten even more. Sean had insisted on delivering her to the café for her performance, and arranged to take her home again, but Gray had coolly usurped him, announcing that *he* would give her a lift home and that there was no point in arguing. Karen had stood mutely by, torn between the possessive need she saw written on his face— and silently echoing it—and Sean's clear disappointment. But he had barely said a word to her on the journey back to the cottage.

She hadn't a clue what he thought of her performance, and was too nervous to ask. He'd stood silently and impatiently at the back of the room while everybody else enthused about her singing and asked when she'd be back to sing again, and she'd been so flustered that she couldn't even recall what she'd said to anyone.

Unable to contain her emotion a second longer, she slammed down the pottery mugs she'd retrieved from the cupboard and spun round to face him. 'What's wrong? Didn't you like my singing? I didn't force you to come and hear me, you know.'

'No... You didn't.'

'Then why are you so—so...?'

'Reticent to pour praise in your ear and tell you how wonderful you were?' His perfectly sculpted lips shaped a sardonic, slightly bitter smile. 'Didn't you have most of the customers in the café falling over themselves to brush up against you just in case you became famous one day? Wasn't that enough adulation to be going on with?'

'I wasn't looking for adulation. Is that what you think?' Her heart bumping in indignation and hurt, Karen sensed her face flood with heat. 'I was surprised you came to hear me at all, if you want to know the truth. I never know what you're going to do—when you're going to show up. When you do I feel like I'm walking on eggshells in case I say the wrong thing. If you had any idea how hard it was for me to play again this afternoon, after all that's happened, then you might have a bit more sensitivity and tact. I certainly wasn't expecting praise. And I don't give a fig about becoming famous! I only got into the music business because of my love of singing. If I can use my talent to earn my living then what could be better? But you know what, Gray? Frankly, I'm not going to waste my time trying to convince you of anything. I've got far better things to do than go down that futile route.'

She would have crossly flounced past him if it weren't for the fact that his hand shot out and held her fast.

'I don't want you to walk on eggshells around me. I'm a morose bastard—I know that. And I don't remotely deserve you even though I want you so badly.'

He sounded so bleak that Karen barely registered the warm grip of his fingers round her wrist. She sighed as she lifted her concerned gaze to examine the misty grey depths of his fascinating eyes, 'You're not a bad person, Gray... A troubled one, maybe... But that doesn't mean you don't deserve happiness or respect. Why do I sense that's what you believe?'

His hold on her slackening, he retrieved his hand and shoved it into the pocket of his jacket. A flicker of some deeply corrosive pain flashed across his handsome face, making his mercurial eyes glitter. 'Why do you think? All the evidence in my life points to the fact that people don't think I'm worth the trouble. Haven't you considered they may be right?'

Before she realised his intention, he'd turned and swept back into the sitting room.

'No,' she said softly, following behind him. 'I've never considered that.'

'Well, then, perhaps you should.'

'I make up my own mind about people.'

'You do, do you?'

'Yes, of course.'

'And I suppose you're never wrong?'

She swallowed across the sudden ache inside her throat—evidence of her sympathy for a man who had built such high walls round himself that even a trained mountaineer would be severely challenged to successfully scale them.

'I'm not wrong about you, Gray.'

'How do you know?'

'I like to think I have good instincts.'

'I'll bet your husband loved that about you.'

'What?'

The man in front of her grimaced. 'Your ability to see the best in people…to forgive.'

Karen shrugged. 'It's just the way I am—but I'm certainly no saint. I have made and still do make lots of mistakes. Ryan was quite aware of my faults, too.'

'And I'll bet he overlooked every single one.'

'Do you want to talk about Ryan, Gray?'

The shake of his head was vehement. 'No. I most definitely *don't* want to talk about him. Do you think I'm some kind of masochist? Just the mere thought that he knew you before I did, held you in his arms before I did, causes me untold agony. He's your past. What I'm interested in is right now.'

Visibly relaxing his shoulders, despite the passion in his voice, he removed his jacket and threw it onto the linen-covered couch. Then he crossed the room to stand in front of her. His warm breath and earthy, masculine scent made Karen tingle right down to the tips of her toes. His long fingers pushed back her hair from her face, then cupped her jaw. *Did she imagine that they shook a little?*

'I really *don't* deserve you. Your singing was outstanding, and your bravery in standing there performing your songs in front of a bunch of strangers even more so. But I'm afraid that if you become too popular your gift will take you away from me, Karen…' He lowered his voice. 'And I'm not ready for that…not yet.'

'I don't want to become popular,' she breathed, losing herself in his intense heated glance, deliberately closing her mind to the words *not yet*. 'I only want to stay here with you.'

His lips descended to bestow the sweetest, most tender kiss he'd ever given her. *It was in that blissful shattering moment that Karen knew she'd lost her heart to Gray O'Connell.* But even amidst her joy in the realisation she recognised the ever-present shadow of potential heartbreak…

'I want to paint you,' he declared, smiling when he lifted his head to study her, repeating his earlier desire and hoping this time her answer would be different. 'Will you come to my house tomorrow and sit for me?'

'Do you mean just a portrait?'

His lips curved in amusement. 'Are you still afraid to take off your clothes for a nude study?'

Blast her unerring ability to blush at the drop of a hat! It was ridiculous, when nearly every night she lay bare in his arms in bed. 'You probably think I'm a dreadful prude.'

'I don't think that at all. I love it that your nature is basically shy. I certainly wouldn't change it, or want you to be any different.'

'In that case, if I agree to sit for you, could we start with a portrait? Just head and shoulders, maybe?'

'A portrait it is, then.' Gray dropped a kiss on the top of Karen's head and grinned.

Bridie Hanrahan heard the frequent thumps and curses emanating from her employer's studio and smiled indulgently. *Something had rattled him.* Rattled him or inspired him, she thought. He'd practically mown her down this morning as he'd torn through the house and up the stairs, yelling out as he went to, 'Make me some strong black coffee would you, Bridie? After that I don't want to be disturbed. I'll be working in my studio all day!'

In that brief encounter the housekeeper had noticed there'd been a light in his eyes that she hadn't ever seen before. If she hadn't bumped into Liz Regan this morning in Eileen's shop then she wouldn't have a clue as to what had put that light there. But after a few minutes' conversation with the young redhead who owned the café she'd learned that Gray O'Connell had turned up yesterday afternoon to hear Karen Ford—the pretty tenant of his father's old cottage—sing.

Bridie was intrigued. The news was akin to hearing that the Pope had dropped into Malloy's Bar and had a couple of pints of Guinness. It was a known fact that Gray didn't socialise...at least not locally, at any rate. He was a regular 'Howard Hughes', and rich as Croesus so the rumour went. But little good his money seemed to have done him so far. He could probably furnish this big old house like Buckingham Palace, but the thought had obviously never even crossed his mind. The man was no doubt still grieving for his father.

Thinking of poor Paddy, and the sad end he had met down there on the beach, Bridie tut-tutted softly, shook her head, then continued along the wide black-and-white tiled hallway to the kitchen to make Gray his coffee.

Sketches of Karen fairly flew off the point of his pencil. Again he worked from pure imagination and memory, which for an artist wasn't entirely satisfactory, but soon, he told himself, he would be working with the real thing. Sheets of smooth cartridge paper were scattered everywhere, and on his easel Gray had stretched and prepared a canvas, ready to start painting when she arrived. At last she had agreed to pose for him. He'd almost held his breath when he'd asked her, fearing that she might say no. Again he found himself moved by her bravery in forging ahead with a new life embracing new experiences and not staying stuck in a grief that anchored her to the past and prevented her from really living.

He could learn a lot from Karen. The woman totally inspired him—and not only with her courage to sing again after the tragedy of her husband's sudden death. One mere glance into her incandescent sky-blue eyes seemed to fill him with an unstoppable flow of energy and excitement. When Gray was lost in her bewitching gaze it helped him forget that he'd been such a terrible disappointment to his father, and that his mother had been too wrapped up in her own misery to hang around and see what he made of his life...

'You've a visitor, Mr O'Connell.'

He was so wrapped up in his thoughts that he didn't even register the fact that his housekeeper stood in the doorway, her florid, kind face somewhat bemused.

'A visitor?' he echoed. He *never* had visitors. The locals knew better than to risk disturbing him. But in the next instant he realised exactly who that visitor was and leapt up off his seat. 'Is it Karen Ford?' he demanded.

'Yes, Mr O'Connell. Shall I bring her up to your studio?'

'Seeing as Miss Ford is sitting for a portrait, then I'd say yes—bring her up to me straight away, Bridie!'

CHAPTER EIGHT

GRAY was seated on a stool, staring out through one of the huge ornate windows that overlooked the sea of rolling green surrounding the house. He cut a lonely, if compelling figure, with his slim but muscular physique, black sweater and familiar tousled black hair. She'd seen him only a few hours ago, yet Karen's heart still bumped against her ribs as if she was seeing him for the very first time.

'The drive up to the house is so long I thought I'd never get here,' she announced nervously, slightly out of breath at the interminable ascent up the staircase with Bridie to the top of the house where Gray's studio was situated.

The open door in sight, she had told his kind-faced housekeeper to go back down. She'd heard the older woman trying to catch her breath behind her, and wondered that she wasn't as skinny as a rake with all the stairs she must regularly have to climb in such a mansion. Even though he'd told her himself that he'd made a fortune, Karen was still overwhelmed at the beauty and size of the great house Gray lived in. He was certainly no starving artist living in a garret! No. Instead, he lived in self-imposed isolated splendour.

The thought made Karen's brows pucker as she glanced round the lofty attic, with its stack of paintings propped up against the walls. His output certainly looked to be prolific. Was his relentless painting the only thing that gave him refuge from pain these days? Even though she ached to examine every canvas, her heart constricted at the thought of him living here alone with just his dog, and seeing only his housekeeper for company.

'The map I drew for you worked out all right, then?'

Her handsome host left his seat to come and greet her, catching her by the elbows to draw her to him. Again she was struck by the chiselled perfection of his extraordinary face. If she were an artist she would beg, borrow or steal for the chance to paint him.

'It was perfect,' she answered.

'No problems understanding it?'

'I presume you're referring to the tired old chestnut that women can't read maps? I actually find it dead easy!'

Gray's generous black brows creased mockingly. 'Is that true?'

'Well...' She couldn't help grinning. 'Not all the time. But you're an expert at drawing, and that's why it was so clear.'

'Carry on in that flattering vein, madam, and you'll go right to the top of my Christmas card list. You might even win yourself a prize.'

Karen loved it when he joked with her like this. When the cloak of brooding darkness that he sometimes wore was laid aside he was a different man entirely. Right now, with Gray in a much lighter frame of mind, it didn't seem as daunting as it had done at first to sit for him and have her portrait painted. At least it would mean time together, she thought wistfully. Time when the words *not yet* could be forgotten for a while and not haunt her...

'Could my prize be permission to look at some of your paintings?' she asked, careful to maintain her light-hearted tone.

It was as though a cloud had streaked across the sun and blotted out the light. 'What for?' Wiping the back of his hand across his mouth, Gray gave her a glance that was guarded, even a little angry. 'So that you can ascertain whether I'm any good or not?'

'It's only natural that I'd be interested in your work, don't you think? Please don't take it the wrong way.'

The light returned—if a little self-consciously. 'Sorry... Old habits die hard, so they say. Do you want to take a look now, or later—after I've made a start on your portrait?'

'Later is fine...thanks.'

'Then in that case we'll crack on, shall we? Here, give me your coat.'

Handing him the duffle coat she'd donned that morning, because there was a distinct wintry snap in the air, Karen watched him stalk across the room to the door, close it, then hang her coat on the single hook behind it—all the while her gaze hypnotised by his taut, firm behind and the long, muscular legs snugly contained in faded worn black denim. He was an artist, but in truth Gray O'Connell was a work of art himself, she thought in silent appreciation.

Releasing a sigh, for the first time she noticed the little puff of steam her warm breath made on the cold air. 'It's chilly in here.' She crossed her arms over the cornflower-blue sweater she wore with her jeans and shivered. 'Don't you feel the cold?'

'Not when I'm lost in my work.'

Returning to her, Gray surprised her by enfolding her in a tight bear hug. In an instant all thought of cold was banished, to be replaced by the most delicious spine-tingling warmth— warmth that made Karen feel like butter melting over hot toast.

'Better?' he teased, lifting his head to smile down at her, two perfectly edible dimples creasing his cheeks.

The man had a smile that could lift a heart so high you never wanted to come down to earth again.

'Much better... Can we stay like this for the rest of the day?' The words were out before she could check them. The thing was, it didn't matter how many nights she spent in Gray's arms—it just never seemed to be enough. *She always craved more.*

The dark pupils engulfed by haunting shades of silvery-grey grew darker still, and his hands dropped to her hips to drag her closer. With his lips just bare inches from hers, Gray intimately lowered his voice. 'Perhaps I was wrong about you being shy? I seem to be uncovering a whole other side to you that leads me to believe you're quite the little seductress.'

'If I am,' Karen breathed softly, 'it's only because you keep putting irresistible temptation in my way.'

'So it's irresistible I am, is it?'

His lips brushed Karen's in a flirtatious, sexy little kiss that made her insides clench and her eyelids drift closed. But right at that moment there was a firm knock at the studio door and they automatically sprang apart. Bridie, pink-cheeked and puffed from her climb up the stairs, opened the door wide to beam at them.

'Sorry to disturb you, Mr O'Connell, but I was wondering if the young lady might like a cup of tea?' she asked brightly.

Karen reddened as Gray's amused glance locked with hers. 'What a perfectly timed entrance, Bridie.' He smiled. 'Not to mention a great idea. Would you like a cup of tea, Karen?' he asked politely, but she saw the corners of his mouth wrestling with the urge to grin, and found herself struggling to keep her expression serious as she turned towards the housekeeper.

'A cup of tea would be lovely, Mrs Hanrahan...thank you.'

'Call me Bridie...everybody else does. Now, what about yourself, Mr O'Connell? Is it coffee you'll be wanting?'

'Coffee would be grand, Bridie,' he agreed, but then he frowned, glanced over at his easel and said, 'But not right now, if you don't mind. Could you bring our drinks up later? Say in about an hour?'

'Of course, Mr O'Connell. That's no trouble at all.'

The door closed and once again Karen found herself alone with Gray.

'No more distractions,' he announced firmly with a glint in his eye. And then suddenly he was all business as he instructed her to sit in the solitary high-backed Victorian armchair by the window. 'I'll put the heater on to keep you warm,' he added.

'Lift your chin a little.' He made a swift practised sketch of her onto the silver-grey backwash he'd painted onto the paper earlier.

As soon as Gray had seen Karen ensconced in the rather grand Victorian armchair it had come to him what a naturally regal air she exuded. Perhaps it was her exquisite bone-structure or her flawless skin, or a combination of both, but she definitely had an intriguing 'touch me not' shimmer that would surely make any man studying the portrait ache to break down that naturally English reserve and make her smile. Unknowingly, he found his own lips twitching.

'What are you grinning at?'

'That's for me to know and you to wonder.'

'So you're going to be cryptic now, are you?'

'Fold your hands in your lap…pretend you're royalty visiting an impoverished but brilliant artist in his lonely garret.'

'What?'

She chuckled, and Gray's insides were suddenly submerged in near volcanic heat. *Did she have any idea how sexy and endearing her laugh was?* How it brought to mind hot butterscotch poured over the creamiest vanilla ice cream?

'That's a stretch! I'm not remotely royal, and neither are you impoverished as far as I can see.' She swept her hand round the lofty proportions of the once grand attic. 'I'm about as un-regal and ordinary as you can get, I assure you. I'm at my happiest baking cakes, singing and playing my guitar.'

'It's true that I'm not impoverished, and you may not be royal, sweetheart, but you have no idea what you've got—and trust me…it's *not* ordinary'

'You're biased.'

'I don't deny it. Sit up! Don't slump in the chair. And if you insist on smiling try for more of a "Mona Lisa" smile rather than a cheeky schoolgirl grin.'

Karen's blue eyes sparkled impishly. 'Are you usually this bossy when you paint someone's portrait?'

Emphasising the clean flowing line of her jaw with his pencil, Gray pursed his lips. 'A man has to lay down the law with a difficult character like you.'

'I'm not difficult.' She gave him a theatrical glare.

Reluctantly, he knew it was time to end the charming banter and get a little more serious. Studying the sketch he'd made for a moment, he drew the small table with his palette on it nearer to the easel and began to block in the figure and background with his brush. Before he'd got very far he glanced over at Karen, noting that her expression had grown pensive.

'I didn't say you had to stop talking,' he remarked gently. 'In fact the bond between the sitter and the artist is a very important factor in creating a good picture. Tell me when you first realised you could sing and what you loved about it.'

'You really want to know about that?'

Gray nodded, but it grieved him that she'd thought he wouldn't be interested. 'Of course.'

'Well…there was always music in the house when I was growing up—mainly because of my dad. He was always playing his records. He loved female vocals best of all, funnily enough.' Her gaze drifted far away for a moment, and Gray elected to stay silent rather than comment. 'I used to sing along.' Her slim shoulders lifted in a shrug. 'He told me my voice was pretty. So I suppose that's when I knew I could sing—when I realised I loved it.'

'And is he still around? Your father, I mean?'

'No. He's not. He died when I was fourteen.' Her hand brushed back her hair.

'Keep still, can you? Let your hair fall back the way it was. That's it.'

Gray stopped painting to study her for a few moments. Her expression wasn't sad, he noted, just resolute. As if she'd *had* to be. But he guessed she'd loved her father very much and clearly still missed him. *Who would be fourteen again, sailing in an untried vessel across the storm-tossed sea that was the experience of most teenagers? Especially when it involved losing a parent,* he reflected sombrely. Although he had grown up with his father, it hadn't made it any easier for Gray to lose him as an adult…especially when his mother was already off the scene. Touching upon the subject even momentarily made his gut twist with pain. It also prompted him to ask Karen about her own mother.

Her expression seemed a little pained as she replied, 'She's still here. Still determined to pretend everything in the garden's lovely, no matter what's going on. She would have made a first-class actress.'

Letting out a long, slow breath, with the tip of a slim sable brush Gray coloured in the dark golden lashes on the beautiful face clearly emerging on the easel in front of him.

'She wasn't supportive when your husband died?'

'Being supportive isn't her forte. She likes to be the Queen Bee—the pivot that the rest of the world revolves around. She also holds the firm belief that families should close ranks when disaster strikes and put on a brave face. They certainly shouldn't let on by word or deed that they're devastated, or act like they need help. That would really let the side down.'

'And you're her only child?'

'Yes.' The blue eyes appeared downcast for a moment. 'Personally, I would have loved to have had a brother or sister, but my mother told me early on that having me had been far too exhausting for her to consider having any more children.'

'So you're not close, then?'

'Not remotely. I mean, I love her—and I think she loves me—but...'

She fell silent for what seemed like a long time. Gray was working on her hair now, trying to capture the little flecks of golden light that the watery sun beaming in through the window brought into arresting focus. *From where was the masochistic impulse coming then to get her to talk about her husband?* He hardly knew. But he saw the surprise and shock in Karen's eyes when he voiced it. 'Tell me about Ryan,' he said.

'What do you want to know?' The lovely blue eyes were distinctly wary.

'Where did you meet him?'

The tip of his paintbrush shaped colour and texture on the canvas as if steered by some unseen force of its own. In her lap, Karen's slim hands unfolded restlessly, then quickly folded again.

'It was at a friend's housewarming. Ryan was an acquaintance of my friend's husband. At the end of the evening some-one—probably after too much wine—suggested we all do a turn. I didn't have my guitar with me, so when it came to my turn I sang a very simple unaccompanied folk song. Later, when we were having coffee, Ryan came over to talk to me and complimented me on my voice. Before I left that night he'd asked me out.'

'And what did he do for a living?'

'He worked in music management.'

'So that's when your career in music took off?'

'Obviously not straight away... But I'd been writing my own songs for quite a while, and along with my voice he thought they had potential.'

Her quizzical glance examined Gray for a moment, as if she were trying to work out where he was coming from. Gray had to privately own to feeling a little discomfited by it.

'Why are you asking me about all this?' she asked. 'I got the distinct impression that under no circumstances did you want to talk about Ryan.'

'I don't...not really. But I am interested in *you*. The fact that you were married to someone else before you met me and that he died isn't something I can easily sweep under the carpet, no matter how much I might secretly want to. I want to know what's shaped you, Karen, what's made you the woman you are. If I can't ask questions about your past, how am I supposed to find these things out?'

'I could turn that question around and ask you the same thing.'

Now Gray *was* uncomfortable. He'd voluntarily led himself down a blind alley from which he couldn't easily escape. 'You know who I am,' he muttered, irritably shoving back the stray lock of black hair that fell against his brow.

'How can you say that? Apart from that rainy night when you turned up at the cottage for the first time you've hardly spoken about yourself at all. I get the distinct impression that your own past is strictly off-limits.'

'Well...you should know by now that I'm not the kind of man that feels the need to spill his guts to all and sundry.'

'Am I "all and sundry", then?' It was with faint alarm that Gray saw the film of moisture hazing Karen's beautiful eyes. He laid down his brush with a sigh.

'You must know you mean more to me than that.'

'I don't know any such thing at all. So tell me...what *do* I

mean to you, Gray? Am I just someone you turn to occasionally to keep the demons away?'

He winced. 'I thought you said that all you wanted was for
me to keep out the cold for a little while? Are you telling me
now that you want something more than that?'

She swallowed hard, shaking her head. 'I don't know... I'm
confused *and* a little scared about it all, if you want to know
the truth.'

Karen had given him an in—an opportunity to really open
up for once and share his doubts and fears and maybe his
hopes, too—but Gray didn't take it.

'Then perhaps we'd better drop the subject and just get on
with what we're doing.'

'Fine... That suits me.'

His lovely model sucked in a breath and a strained little
smile touched her lips. He could tell it didn't suit her at all to
drop the subject, and again Gray deplored his lack of courage
and sensitivity in not having a proper discussion about the
matter. But realistically he already knew that Karen deserved
far better than him. Why not just be grateful for her being in
his life right now and stop muddying the waters by fantasising
about a future that would never, *could* never be his?

He resumed his painting in silence, and shortly after that
tense little episode Bridie arrived with their refreshments.
As Gray invited Karen to bring her tea and come and survey
the stunningly impressive view from the huge pre–Palladian
windows, he found himself longing to make things right between them again.

'Is there anything else you need back at the cottage?'

'I've got everything I need, so no. But thanks for asking'

'Are you sure?'

'Yes, I'm sure.'

'You can have anything you want, you know? Hell, I'd even
pull the place down and build a new house for you right on

the spot if you wanted.' His long fingers tightened in agitation round his coffee mug.

Her gaze perturbed, Karen turned to look at him. 'Why would you do that, Gray? Pull down your father's cottage, I mean?'

He felt a little desperate for a moment. 'Until you came it held too many unhappy memories for me... I don't even know why I decided to rent it out in the first place. I wouldn't be sorry to see it pulled down.'

'I understand how you would feel that way, but I'm personally very glad that you did decide to rent it out. I like it there very much. As for suggesting you build a new house—I don't even know how long I'll be staying. Right now the cottage suits me fine just as it is.'

'I want—I *need* to give you something...don't you understand?' Plucking the mug out of her hand, Gray placed it on the windowsill next to his own. Inside his chest his heart was racing as he gripped her hands to stare long and hard into her beautiful upturned face. 'And don't even *think* about leaving... not for a long, long time.'

'There *is* something you can give me.' Withdrawing one of her hands from his clasp, Karen gently touched the side of his beard-shadowed jaw. 'You can give me a promise that you'll start to think better of yourself and allow a little happiness into your life from time to time. Can you do that, Gray?'

As he met that mesmerising warm gaze, emotion ambushed Gray and he wanted to hold on to her for the longest time. But, true to form, such a strong sensation of need scared him, too. It wasn't his style to need anybody...at least not in a way that made them essential to his life and happiness...

'I'll try,' he answered, his smile awkward, almost as if it didn't fit his face.

'Good.' Karen's smile was much more natural. 'Will you show me some of your paintings now?'

'Sure…why not?'

Dropping down onto her haunches to examine a breath-taking landscape of verdant emerald hills rolling down to a stormy sea at sunset, Karen surveyed the stunning skill of the artist in amazement. She'd hardly known what to expect when it came to Gray's work, but she knew she'd anticipated nothing half as good or tremendous as this.

'This is incredible. It's got so much presence you can almost breathe the wind-blown air and hear the waves crashing,' she commented. 'And that fiery red and gold sunset…it stirs the heart, Gray.' She could almost *sense* him moving awkwardly behind her, as if the compliment unsettled him—unsettled him and probably made him inwardly deny it, she guessed.

'I did that one about a year ago,' he murmured. 'Chase and I came upon the scene one evening during one of our long walks. Luckily I had my sketchpad with me at the time.'

'It's clear you enjoy painting landscapes,' Karen murmured, rising to her feet and carefully going through the stack of work behind the painting she'd been examining.

'I do.'

'You don't do many portraits, then?' She halted her study of the paintings to give her full attention to the man waiting beside her.

'Not very often.'

'Is there a particular reason why?'

'I don't care to have people coming to the house.' Lifting a shoulder, he glanced away.

'Then I'm honoured that you asked me.'

'Are you fishing for a compliment?'

'Do I need to fish?' she teased.

'No.'

The grey eyes that had the haunting quality of the sea in them were so intense for a moment that Karen felt as though she was melting in the heat they emitted.

'No, you do not.'

Heart clonking against her ribs, she blurted, 'How come your pictures aren't framed and displayed all over the house? It seems a shame to keep them up here, just gathering dust. People would love to see them, I'm sure.'

'You mean the same people that don't come to the house?'

'Even so, you should display them out of respect for yourself. I'd certainly enjoy seeing them, and so I'm sure would Bridie. Why not get them framed and put up? I'll help you if you like.'

'I'll think about it.'

Karen got the distinct impression that he wouldn't. But now she was a woman on a mission—a mission to get this talented and wounded man to wake up to his own potential, to leave his traumatic past behind and enjoy the one thing he was clearly passionate about, the thing that could open doors to a new and more fulfilling future...even if that future didn't include *her*.

'You'd better finish your tea. I need to get back to work on the portrait. The light will be fading in another couple of hours, and I'd like to get as much done as possible.'

Already moving back towards his easel, Gray didn't glance round to see if Karen followed him. It seemed as though he was retreating behind that protective wall again—the wall that made Karen feel as if he would only invite her so far into his private enclave before putting her safely at a distance again.

Folding her arms across her chest, she sighed. Now she *did* have his attention.

'What's wrong?'

'Don't you think we should get some air? Take Chase for a walk, perhaps?'

'We will after I've finished working on the portrait for the day... Are you getting bored already, sitting for me?'

'No. I suppose I'm just a little restless.'

She found herself on the disturbingly arousing end of one of his rare melting smiles.

'Restless and beautiful... It's a good title for your portrait.'

'If you say so.' She made a face at him.

'I do. Now, get your pretty little butt over here and sit for me—before I find a strap and tie you to the chair!'

Her skin burning at the very idea, Karen couldn't even find words in her scrambled brain to reply...

CHAPTER NINE

'MY CHEF Jorge made the coffee. He trained as a barista in Italy, and I kid you not—it's to die for!' Liz Regan beamed at Karen across a table at the back of the closed café as the two women sat together for a coffee and 'a cosy little chat', as she had put it to Karen.

Happy to count the enthusiastic redhead as a new friend, Karen took a sip of the fragrant cappuccino in front of her and briefly squeezed her eyes shut in pleasure. 'You're right…it's divine. Where on earth did you find this Jorge?'

The sparkly green eyes of the other woman effervesced even more. 'I met him on holiday in Majorca last year. He's Spanish. To tell you the truth he was planning on working in the UK, but I very cheekily enticed him away from that idea and persuaded him to come to Ireland and work for me instead.'

Karen grinned, sensing there was more. 'And?'

'Winters here can be grim. A woman needs a fit and active male to help keep her warm at nights. Call it clever strategic planning on my part, as well as unashamed self-interest.'

It didn't escape Karen that Liz had used a similar phrase to Gray's, when he had promised to 'keep out the cold' for her for a while. She fell silent, thinking about last night and the heat they had generated again in bed after they'd agreed he'd follow her home to the cottage. Once again, Gray had left her in the early hours of the morning to return home...

'And what about you, Karen?' The redhead leaned across the cheerful yellow tablecloth with a knowing glint. 'It can't have escaped your notice that everybody was very much surprised when our local Heathcliff himself turned up the other afternoon to hear you sing...feeling up to spilling the beans?'

It was inevitable, Karen supposed, that sooner or later someone was going to quiz her about Gray. But it didn't mean she was ready or even *wanted* to discuss it with anyone... even Liz.

'No, not really.' She shrugged, shielding both her gaze and her feelings briefly behind her mug of coffee.

Running her fingers through her cropped red hair, Liz grimaced. 'I know you probably don't want to say anything in deference to him, and I'm sure you think we're all a bunch of dreadful nosy parkers, but the people here are still very sympathetic towards Gray O'Connell, and at the end of the day we look after our own. His father Paddy was well-liked, and everyone was shocked and saddened when he died. Not only had Gray to deal with the trauma of that, but then his flighty girlfriend Maura left him for his best friend and ran away with him to Canada—we could all see how he turned in on himself and became a virtual recluse. It's not natural for a fit, handsome man like him... To be alone, I mean...'

Her insides churning, Karen was trying hard to process the startling revelation that Gray had had a girlfriend who'd left him to run off with his best friend. *Was that the reason he seemed so wary about committing to a proper relationship or discussing anything personal?* Who could blame him, when it seemed that anyone he'd ever cared about had abandoned him? Under the circumstances it was hardly a surprise that he kept everyone at arm's length and chose to isolate himself. If only he'd told her about what had happened with this Maura—even though it would be excruciating for her to hear about another woman and even harder to imagine Gray suffering because he'd lost her.

'We're just…good friends,' she explained—without conviction, it had to be said. But how could she tell Liz anything else when she was too scared to trust that her passionate and volatile relationship with Gray might last?

'Good friends, is it?' The other girl's eyes easily transmitted her doubt.

Distressed, Karen moved her head from side to side. 'To tell you the truth,' she admitted, heart pounding because Liz looked to be hanging on her every word, 'I'm mad about him. I'm mad about him even though I have this terrible fear that he'll tell me goodbye almost every time we meet. There…' She blinked back the moisture that surged into her eyes and shuddered. 'The thing is I never expected to fall so hard for someone so soon after losing Ryan…my husband. I think I'm still in shock about what's happened between me and Gray.'

'What was your marriage like?' the other girl asked thoughtfully. 'Did you fall for Ryan as hard as you've fallen for Gray?'

Feeling guilty and wretched, Karen sighed softly. 'No,' she whispered, 'I didn't. He was my best friend—the one I could turn to when I was unhappy or hurt—the person who was always there for me.'

'But the sparks didn't exactly fly in bed?' Liz smiled gently.

Blue eyes enormous, Karen stared. 'How did you guess?'

'It's not uncommon…a girl thinking that she should marry her best male friend and then finding out when the deed is done that she's made a mistake.'

'Ryan was never a mistake!'

'I'm sure he wasn't, Karen—but the fact that you've fallen

so hard for Gray suggests that you weren't really in love with Ryan. Don't look so shocked… He was still your best friend and you loved him—just not in the same way that you love Gray O'Connell. Passion is never neat and tidy, you know. It rarely ticks all the right boxes and behaves itself as people think it should. And when it descends your whole world is turned on its head and won't ever be the same again.'

Reflecting on the other woman's unexpectedly revelatory words, Karen touched her hand to her forehead, imagining her heartbeat sounded like crashing waves slamming against rocks in her ears. 'How do you know all this? Did it happen to you?'

'Yes…when I was working in London for a hotel chain in the west end. He was a visiting CEO from Australia, and he came to the hotel for a meeting. I served him his coffee, our eyes met, and that was it… *Wham!* I felt like I'd been hit by a cyclone.'

'But it didn't work out between the two of you?'

'No.' The redhead winced. 'It didn't. But right now we're talking about you, not me.'

'I expect you think I'm an awful fool, falling for someone as emotionally unavailable and damaged as Gray.'

Reaching across the table, Liz gave Karen's hand a sympathetic squeeze. 'You're not a fool, sweetheart. Far from it. But it sounds to me like you didn't have much choice in the matter of the fascinating Mr O'Connell. Sure, hasn't he got it all? He's tall, dark, handsome—and has a tragic past. We women seem hard-wired to fall for the wounded ones, don't we? Plus he has an air of mystery about him that would tempt any woman with an ounce of curiosity in her blood to try and unravel what makes him tick. But, passion aside, I won't pretend I'm not concerned about how you'll cope if what you have together should suddenly come to an end.'

'I'll manage…I'll have to. It's not as though I've never had

to deal with the sudden end of a relationship before, is it? It's
a risk every woman takes when she falls for a man...that he'll
end up hurting her, I mean.'

'True. But losing your heart to a man who can't or won't
give you his love in return because he's built a fortress round
his own heart to protect himself... Well, that's no easy path,
for sure. Be good to yourself, Karen. That's my advice. Take
one step at a time and keep something back just in case it
doesn't work out as you might hope.'

Karen didn't reply, because a numbing wave of dread was
washing through her at the realisation that she didn't have a
hope of 'keeping something back'—because she'd already
given everything she had in her to Gray.

'In the meantime—' her companion smiled warmly '—I
want you to know that I'm your friend as well as your sometimes employer, and I won't be blabbing any of what you've
told me to a soul. Not even my brother Sean...who, by the
way, has quite a thing for you.'

'He has?' Dismayed, Karen crumpled her smooth brow.

'Yes, he has—even more so since he heard you sing. He
swears you've the voice of an angel, and I'm inclined to agree.
You won't be singing for me for long before some bigwig
music executive gets to hear about you via the local tom-tom
drums and tempts you away with a record deal, I'm sure! We
may be situated in the back of beyond, but news of a talent
like yours travels fast. But, that aside, Sean's seen the way
it is between you and Gray O'Connell, and he won't make a
nuisance of himself.'

Thinking of the afternoon she'd spent with Gray yesterday,
having her portrait painted and looking through his sublime
landscape paintings, Karen realised how much she'd been
hoping for some sign from him that he considered them to
be in a proper relationship—a relationship that truly meant
something to him. His passionate admission that he wanted

to do something for her...that he *needed* to do something for her...had honestly taken her aback. But she knew it didn't mean he was any closer to wanting some kind of real commitment, and she couldn't prevent the sense of desolation that arose inside her at that.

Her astute companion picked up on her despondency straight away. 'You need a night out, my girl,' she announced enthusiastically. 'You need to have yourself some fun and forget about Gray O'Connell for a while. It's Sean's birthday tomorrow, and I'm throwing him a party here at the Cantina. I was going to ask if you wouldn't mind playing some music, as well as joining us with a few friends in some dancing and a few laughs...how about it?'

A party... Since when had the concept become so alien to her? Karen wondered. When had it become something to fear instead of an event she could enjoy?

'Hey!' Her emerald eyes twinkling mischievously, Liz reached forward to playfully slap her on the arm. 'Don't you dare tell me you can't remember how to have fun. If you do, then I'll just have to help refresh your memory in any way that I can—and I'm warning you...I don't take any prisoners!'

Gray swept into Karen's sitting room that evening with a preoccupied glance that didn't bode well, and as she shut the door on the seemingly perpetual icy rain that filled the night behind him she deliberately gave him one of her most welcoming smiles.

'Hi. I see you've brought the rain with you again...must be a knack.'

Crossing to the hearty blaze in the fireplace, as was his habit, Gray held out his hands to its warmth for a few moments before turning to reply, 'Yeah, it's a knack, all right. Bad weather seems to follow me around, right enough.'

'What's wrong?'

'Nothing.' The smile he tried hard for made Karen want to weep. 'Would you make me some coffee?'

'Of course... I've been baking. I've made a Victoria sponge. Shall I cut you a slice?'

'No cake. Just coffee...thanks'

Moving to the door again, he shucked off his wet jacket and hung it on the hook there. About to turn away to the kitchen, Karen felt her heart skip a beat when he caught her and pulled her gently but firmly against his hard lean body. His hands were cold as winter, as were his sweater and jeans, and his handsome sculpted visage glistened with droplets of icy rain and his arresting silvery eyes crinkled at the corners.

'No matter what the weather's like outside, you always remind me of sunshine.'

His voice was the sensual equivalent of smooth Irish whiskey and a crackling log fire. The disturbingly arousing combination made Karen melt. A muscle contracted in the side of his cheek just before he lowered his face to hers and kissed her. His lips were cool as a sheet of cold glass, but almost immediately heat and hunger broke through to warm them and his silken tongue swept the soft contours of her mouth as if she was fresh clean air he desperately needed to breathe.

Karen's knees all but crumpled. But, while she ached to lose herself in the magic of Gray's kisses and the unfailing seductive touch of his hands, she sensed that beneath his raw and hungry need for her something had upset him. *She wanted to know the reason.* Slowing the kiss, gradually moving her lips away, she cupped his unshaven jaw between her hands, staring concernedly up into the long-lashed, depthless grey eyes.

'Something's bothering you. Won't you tell me what it is?' she urged softly.

Sometimes it was hard for Gray to think straight when his gaze tumbled into Karen's. It was so easy to just get lost in that flawless sea of blue for the longest time. But his heart constricted for a different reason at her question. Dropping his hands from around her slender shapely hips, he restlessly moved away. His chilled fingers tunnelled through his mane of damp black hair.

'It's the anniversary of my father's death,' he explained dully. 'I visited his grave today.'

'Oh, Gray. I would have come with you if you'd said.'

'It wouldn't have helped. No matter how hard I try, I just can't forget what happened to him...the way he died out there alone on the beach. I revisit the scene over and over again in my mind, trying to make right how it ended, trying to come to terms and accept it—but how can it ever be right? It was a mess...a bloody mess! Living with the legacy of it just seems to get harder as time goes by...the pain doesn't lessen. Maybe it's because the old devil never forgave me for leaving? For not helping him keep the farm?'

'That's just a story, Gray...a fantasy. You don't know that it's true. Nobody can know what was in your father's mind when he died. You'd returned, hadn't you? You returned because you wanted to make amends...he must have known that.'

It was true that Paddy had been glad to see him, Gray remembered. But it had only taken a few minutes before he'd glimpsed the defeat and disappointment in his eyes, too. How was he supposed to reconcile that?

'I offered to set him up with a new farm,' he said out loud to Karen. 'Offered to pay for any amount of hired help to make it work. But he told me it was too late for that. He was too old and too tired, he said, and he didn't have the heart for it any more.'

'Even so, I can't believe for a moment that your father would have wanted you to feel as wretched as you still do about his death. You did your best by him, Gray. He may have wanted you to stay and help run the farm, as his father had done before him, but that doesn't mean it was the right thing for you. At the end of the day your father made his own choices and so did you. We all do. That's not a crime.'

Suddenly Karen was in front of him, her gaze spilling over with tenderness and concern. For the life of him Gray couldn't think what he'd done to attract such heartfelt regard.

'And I'm certain that whatever happened between you he'd want you to forget it and leave the past behind,' she insisted. 'Yes, leave it behind—so that you can live the present to the full. You have every means of doing that. You've got the resources and you've got your talent for painting. So why not concentrate on all the things you've got in your favour, make a new start and try to enjoy life again?'

He so wanted to believe that what she said was possible. Part of him was furious with himself for wallowing...for not just counting his blessings and vowing to make the most of his life as Karen suggested. But the ghosts of the past wouldn't easily let him go. Their clammy touch crawled up his spine whenever he was alone in that great mausoleum of a house, mocking him and making him despise the man he'd become. The only light on the horizon was the beautiful blue-eyed angel who stood in front of him. But what right did Gray have to embroil her in his troubles? Hadn't she suffered enough with her own tragic loss?

The great need to do something wonderful for her, to do something purely for her enjoyment and pleasure, arose inside him again.

Catching her hands, he tugged her towards him. 'Come away with me for a few days.'

'What?' Her expression was genuinely stunned.

'Come away with me to Paris. I have an apartment there, in the Rue Saint-Honoré. I haven't been there in quite a while, but there's an agency that takes care of it for me. All I have to do is make a phone call.'

'You have a place in Paris?'

'I do. We'll go tomorrow. What do you say?'

'Tomorrow?' she echoed.

To Gray's immense disquiet, Karen freed her hands, then crossed her arms over the front of her dress. The material was a soft plum-coloured jersey and it fitted her eye-catching figure to perfection, hugging her breasts and hips just as he longed to mould his hands to them himself. But as she studied him her glance was torn.

'I can't go tomorrow.'

'Why?'

'I've had an invitation. An invitation that I've already accepted.'

'And who might that be from?'

'Liz Regan. She's throwing a party at the café tomorrow night.'

Unable to conceal the crushing disappointment that welled up inside him, Gray knew his reply sounded accusing and unreasonable. 'So you'd rather go to this party than come away with me?'

'I didn't say that. But if I make a promise I like to keep it. Liz also asked me to sing. Anyway, I'll go and make your coffee.'

As she turned towards the kitchen Gray followed her. 'What's it in aid of, this party that you're so keen to attend?'

Straight away he saw the scarlet tinge that flooded into her otherwise pale cheeks.

'It's to celebrate her brother Sean's birthday,' she answered, coming to a sudden standstill before him.

Just the sound of the other man's name on her lips cut him to the quick. Inside his chest, his heart rioted. 'What is it about

Sean Regan that you find so irresistible?' he demanded with a snarl.

'I don't find him irresistible. Why do you always have to jump to such ridiculous conclusions?'

'Obviously I wasn't invited as well?'

The slender well-shaped brows on the beautiful face before him lifted in surprise. 'Would you have gone if you had been?'

'Of course I wouldn't. But it still galls me to think that you'll be there, singing and helping to entertain that young pup, when you could have gone to Paris with me instead.'

'You're being completely unreasonable, and I'm sure you know it. Why can't we go to Paris the day after tomorrow?'

Gray shrugged, unable to keep a lid on his temper. 'Because I've already decided I want to go tomorrow. I'm not going to change my mind simply to pander to the whims of a woman!' he answered furiously. 'The sooner you realise that, the better off we'll be.'

'Is that why your previous girlfriend Maura walked out on you?' Karen came back at him, her skin flushed and her blue eyes glinting. 'Because you were so selfish and unreasonable that she finally couldn't tolerate living with you any longer?'

The shock of her words was like iced water being poured down his back. Not because Gray had even *cared* that Maura had left, but because Karen was more or less telling him that she wasn't surprised that a woman would leave him. *Who had told her about Maura?* he wondered. He quickly dismissed it as unimportant. Half the town would know his sorry history. But it still stung that the woman he respected more than any other clearly thought him a poor bargain. That hurt more than a thousand scores across his heart.

'Forget the damn coffee,' he muttered, grabbing his leather

jacket off the coat hook and flinging angrily out through the door into the bitterly cutting chill of the rainy night...

Dressing for the party the following evening, Karen went over and over again in her mind the way Gray had stormed out of the cottage the previous night. At first she'd mentally cursed the rash, angry words she'd thrown at him about Maura, had wanted to chase after him and tell him how sorry she was. She didn't mean it, she'd say, but he had goaded her into retaliating when he'd said he didn't pander to the whims of a woman. Was she so unimportant and inconsequential to him that any suggestions or preferences she might have were instantly to be dismissed?

Calming herself down, she had been struck that maybe Gray needed to mull over the idea that he was selfish and unreasonable. It couldn't hurt to stand her ground and hope he would reflect and take stock, could it? But what if she'd gone too far? What if he decided to end what they had there and then and wouldn't see or speak to her ever again?

In the middle of applying her lipstick in front of the bathroom mirror, Karen suddenly felt quite nauseous.

Blinking back the hot tears that surged into her eyes, she wished she wasn't going to the party—wished she'd declined or, if not that, agreed to go to Paris with Gray and explained later to Liz why she hadn't shown up for Sean's birthday. *Blast!* Now she'd have to do her make-up all over again. She looked like a sad clown, with black mascara streaking down her face. *Yesterday had been the anniversary of his father's death*, she recalled painfully. And she'd heartlessly left him alone with his grief, his guilt, and no doubt his self-loathing, too...

The groan that left her lips might have been that of some wounded animal. The idea that she'd never see him again, or that he might pass her in the street or down on the beach and ignore her, made her feel physically ill. Karen had broken her heart over Ryan's sudden unexpected death, but her grief then was nothing to the agony that gripped her now at the idea of losing Gray…

He'd spent the night in front of the fire, brooding and drinking whiskey. Eventually he'd succumbed to a heavy troubled sleep in the armchair, and woken in the early hours of the morning with his body aching as if he'd been trampled and kicked by a mule and to the cold grey ashes of the fire. Making his way upstairs to bed, he'd yanked the covers over him and cursed himself soundly for behaving like some ill-mannered oaf last night. When he'd recalled Karen's angry, crestfallen face when he'd made that infantile comment about not pandering to a woman's whims he'd had the blackest moment, feeling certain he'd screwed up the one chance he had to bring some peace and happiness back into his life.

Getting up and moving across the room, he had opened the windows wide and gulped in some long deep breaths of the frosted early-morning air. At last he'd managed to wrench his thoughts away from his tormenting introspection and had found himself mulling over his painting instead. When the surprising urge to try and rebuild his life and make a fresh start had come unexpectedly to him he'd been filled with such a surge of renewed energy that he had urgently got dressed and gone straight to his studio…

'Thanks very much.' Gray shook the stout sandy-haired picture-framer's callused hand at the front door as he prepared to leave. 'You've done a grand job.'

'Any time, Mr O'Connell. It's been a pleasure doing business with you, so it has. If there's ever any more paintings you'd like framed, don't hesitate to give me a call.' The man thoughtfully scratched his head beneath his flat dog-tooth cap.

'That's some talented artist who's painted those pictures. Are you acquainted with him or her, by any chance?'

'Why? Do you want to buy one?'

'Sure, I wish I could afford to, Mr O'Connell, but a picture-framer's wages don't stretch to buying great works of art, I'm afraid!'

Suppressing a highly amused guffaw...*great works of art, indeed...!* Gray reflected on the surprisingly fulfilling morning he'd had, selecting the paintings he wanted framed. At times he'd wrestled with displaying them at all, but there'd been other times when Karen's heartfelt encouragement not to hide his work away had spurred him on. Why had it taken him so long to realise that she was right about that? *She'd been right about a lot of things,* he reflected ruefully... He'd had the worst night he'd had in ages after leaving her last night—*deservedly so.* When he saw her next he would tell her why.

It had been midmorning when he'd rung the local picture-framers and told them he wanted to employ them straight away. After being told they had a list of commissions to see to before they could get to him, Gray had cut through the 'Well, now, I don't know...' and ums and ahs and offered them an eye-watering fee they couldn't refuse.

All in all it had been a good day's work, and he couldn't believe the time when he finally glanced at his watch. It was almost time for dinner, and going by the delicious aroma wafting out of the kitchen Bridie was making one of her tantalising and hearty stews. Walking past the line of paintings he'd hung in the long downstairs corridor that led to the kitchen at the end, he glanced at them critically, but with some satisfaction, too, as he passed.

What would Karen think about what he'd done? he mused. She'd been hovering on the edges of his mind all day, and every time he conjured up her beautiful face Gray's gut would painfully clench with longing. He ached to hold and kiss her and tell her how sorry he was for being such an out-and-out swine—so sorry that he was willing to *beg* her forgiveness if she seemed hesitant to give it. At any rate, after eating his meal he fully intended on going down into the town to discreetly set up a watch on Liz's Cantina, wait for Karen to leave the party, and hopefully convince her to come home with him tonight. It hardly bore contemplating that she might reject his plea and tell him to go to hell...

CHAPTER TEN

THE party was still in full swing when Karen realised that she'd had enough and wanted to leave. She'd enjoyed singing the uplifting tunes she'd performed for Sean, his sister and assembled friends, but as for dancing and engaging with the other guests in conversation—well, she'd found that increasingly hard when her heart was weighed down with anxious musings about Gray.

Weaving her way through the hotly perspiring bodies gyrating to the latest hip-hop sounds, she located Liz near the back of the room, with her Spanish boyfriend and chef Jorge, and started to make her apologies.

'You're not leaving?' the redhead exclaimed, clearly disappointed. 'It's not even late yet, and tomorrow's Sunday. You can lie in all day if you want. Come on, my pretty little songbird, have another drink and let your hair down for once.'

She could see that her vivacious employer in her pink satin party dress and flashing green earrings was more than a little intoxicated as she leaned against her well-built Spanish boyfriend, and Karen was quite glad that she'd stuck with fruit juice and hadn't succumbed to alcohol—apart from champagne to wish Sean a happy birthday. Aside from the fact she had to drive herself home to the cottage, she was determined to keep a clear head to think about her future.

Serious misgivings about the wisdom of staying in Ireland were arising—misgivings she couldn't deny.

She was no longer sure it was the best thing for her, because if Gray ended their relationship then what was the point? She honestly didn't believe she could cope with bumping into him, knowing the passion they'd shared was no more. Or—worse—maybe seeing him with someone else.

Leaning forward, Karen planted an affectionate peck on Liz's cheek. 'I don't want another drink, thanks. I've had a great time, but now I'm going home. I'll see you next week… enjoy the rest of your weekend, won't you?'

'What about Sean?'

'What *about* Sean?' Karen echoed, bewildered. The last she'd seen of Liz's handsome young brother he'd been dancing with a pretty brunette who—going by her entranced expression—was completely enthralled by him. Now, glancing over the bobbing heads of the dancers on the floor, she failed to spy his tousled fair head anywhere.

'I'm a bit concerned about him. For someone celebrating his birthday he's a little too down in the dumps for my liking,' the redhead asserted. 'Do me a favour before you go, will you, Karen? See if he's outside, and if he is wish him a happy birthday again…it would mean a lot, coming from you. See if you can cheer him up a bit. Thanks, my friend…and thanks, too, for your wonderful singing.'

The sharp cold air that hit her as she opened the door to step outside had never been more welcome. At last Karen could breathe freely again, without the impediment of the muggy heat inside and the inevitable fumes of alcohol. Standing her guitar up against the brick wall, she tied the wraparound-style jacket she'd donned over slim black trousers and a matching sleeveless top, and almost jumped out of her skin when Sean peeled out of the shadows to greet her. She saw him flick the cigarette he'd been smoking into the alleyway next to the building. His green eyes were instantly warm as they alighted on her.

'It's a bit like a sauna in there, isn't it?' He smiled. 'Much better out here. You're not going home?'

'I'm afraid I am,' she answered, swiftly checking the urge to ask him where the pretty brunette had disappeared to, in case it was the worst thing to say because she'd left him. 'I know you probably think I'm extremely boring, but I'm actually feeling quite tired.'

It wasn't a lie, Karen thought sadly. Emotion—particularly *negative* emotion—was apt to sap her energy, and she'd experienced enough emotion to drain her dry since Gray had walked out on her last night.

'I'd never think you were boring in a million years, Karen.' As he stepped a little closer to her, Sean's expression changed subtly to become more serious. 'If you want to know the truth, I think you're pretty incredible.'

Embarrassed, Karen shrugged. 'That's sweet of you...even if I can't agree.'

'It made my birthday, you coming to sing for me. I could listen to you sing every night if I had the choice.'

The next step he took towards her brought his body mere inches away from hers. He was so close that the almost overpowering scent of his strong cologne made her wince.

Feeling suddenly uneasy, Karen pushed back her hair and furnished him with an uncertain smile. 'Well...happy birthday again, Sean—and thanks for setting me up with the amp and everything. No doubt I'll see you around...probably at Liz's some time.'

When she would have moved away, Sean reached out to touch his hand to the back of her waist. In the next instant she felt herself drawn towards him. The kiss he'd clearly intended for her lips clumsily dropped against the side of her cheek as

Karen quickly realised his aim and stepped away, her heart drumming hard as she reached for her guitar.

'Don't go,' he implored, expression contrite. 'I didn't mean to offend you—but you just look so beautiful tonight that I couldn't resist trying to steal a kiss. Can't we go back inside and at least have a drink together, maybe share a dance?'

'I don't think that would be a good idea, Sean.'

'Karen!'

The sound of a heartrendingly familiar voice coming from the shadows of the small car park across the road almost made her knees buckle with relief. But at the same time Karen was confused. *What was Gray doing here? Surely he hadn't been waiting for her?*

As she peered into the night his dark, imposing figure emerged from the gloom to be highlighted by a streetlamp. He was dressed completely in black. The droplets of rain glinting off his leather jacket and ebony hair sparkled like tiny gemstones beneath the lamp's yellow glare, and made him look like the brooding hero of some cinematic thriller. She froze, torn between running across the road and throwing herself into his arms or moving directly towards her car and driving home.

'Is everything okay?' In a few long-legged strides he was in front of her, his hands firmly on her arms, his stormy grey eyes burning down into her upturned face as if she was the home he longed to return to.

'I'm fine.' She heard the slight quiver in her voice. 'What are you doing here?'

He didn't answer straight away, just continued to stare at her as if mesmerised. But then he glanced towards Sean, as if suddenly aware of the younger man resentfully watching them.

'Good party was it, Sean?' he mocked, and Karen sensed the held-back fury in him.

Her stomach flipped. *Had he seen the younger man's clumsy attempt at kissing her?* Did he believe she'd encouraged him?

'It was fine,' Sean mumbled, awkwardly digging his hands into his jeans pockets. 'It's still going on. Do you fancy coming in for a drink?'

'No, thanks.' His mouth tight, Gray reached for Karen's guitar, then slipped his hand possessively into hers. 'Me and the lovely lady here are going home... Oh, and Sean?'

'What is it?'

'Next time you want to try and kiss some unsuspecting and uninterested woman, make sure it's not Karen...okay?'

'Gray!' Shocked, Karen tried to wrench her hand free, but the man by her side was having none of it.

'He needed to be put straight about us,' he muttered darkly as he led her back across the road to the car park.

Stopping in front of the familiar Range Rover, he opened the passenger door at the back to deposit her guitar on the seat without even asking her. By now she, too, was furious. 'What do you think you're doing?'

'I came to pick you up and take you home,' he announced, slamming the door shut, then turning towards her.

'I don't need you to take me home...I brought my own car. And what do you mean, "He needed to be put straight about us"? Last night you slammed out of the cottage in a temper just because I stood up for myself and wouldn't let you bully me into doing something *you* wanted to do because I'd already committed to coming to Sean's birthday party. Now you're talking about us as if we had some kind of meaningful relationship! Have I missed something, Gray?' Breathing hard, Karen couldn't hold back the tide of emotion that engulfed her.

The man in front of her grimaced painfully. 'First of all, I owe you an apology for the way I lost my temper last night.

Secondly, I want you to know that I wasn't angry with you for saying what you did about Maura leaving me. You had a right to get back at me. But I also want you to know that I felt nothing when she went except relief. For a while she was company for me during a difficult time...when I lost my father, to be exact. But we both knew we neither wanted nor expected a future together. I reacted badly because you seemed to find it so easy to believe that she *would* walk out on me...as if you wouldn't dispute that I must have deserved it.'

Roughly combing his fingers through his hair, Gray furrowed his indomitable brow. 'I don't deny that I was probably hell to live with at the time, and now all I feel for the woman is compassion that she put up with me for as long as she did. I wallowed in grief and guilt for too long, and anyone close to me or who had dealings with me took the brunt of it. I honestly regret that.'

Digesting his frank confession with surprise, and something like hope flooding her heart, Karen breathed out a sigh. 'You didn't love her, then? Maura, I mean?'

'Good God, no... For a while we simply found each other... shall we say convenient?'

Knowing immediately that he meant sexually, she felt a jealous jolt shoot through her like a flame-tipped arrow. 'Oh...'

Gray punctuated the cold night air with a throaty chuckle. 'I'm a man with a healthy libido—I don't deny it. And I'm not going to pretend those needs don't disturb me if they're not met even if admitting it makes you blush, sweetheart.'

Catching her by the waist, he brought Karen's body up close into his lean hard middle, and the chill that was making her shiver fled as though a blazing sun had just appeared in the sky and was shining down on her.

'I owe you an apology, too, Gray. I didn't mean to upset you with what I said. I just reacted in the heat of the moment.'

'Like I said, you had every right to retaliate. It's commend-able that you wanted to honour a promise…I had no right to try and tell you what to do. Was the party good?'

Without you, every minute felt like a lifetime… She didn't say the words out loud, but she longed to. 'It was okay. As it turns out I wasn't really in the mood for a party after all. I would have preferred to have stayed at home.'

'Or gone to Paris with me?' Gray suggested ruefully, the beginnings of a surprisingly tender smile touching his lips.

'Maybe.' Karen dipped her head.

'By the way, was Sean bothering you?' he asked. His tone definitely had an underlying thread of jealousy in it.

'No. I expect he just had one Guinness too many—but then it *is* his birthday.'

Dropping a kiss at the side of her mouth, Gray pulled back to examine her face. 'I expect I'll have to get used to that… men looking at you and lusting after you. But woe betide any man who tries to do more than just look,' he warned.

'That sounds a little possessive.'

His silvery eyes flared. 'That's because I *am* possessive where you're concerned.'

'Well, don't be. I'm human, Gray…not some object you can own like that portrait of me you're painting!'

Karen pushed away from him even before she realised she was going to, swamped with disappointment and hurt that she *still* seemed to mean nothing more to him than the 'con-venient' and unlucky Maura. As much as she loved him, she wouldn't settle for anything less than his love in return. She might be unsure about a lot of things, but she wasn't unsure about that.

Delving into her jacket pocket, her fingers curled round her car keys. 'I'm going home now. Can I get my guitar?' she said with a thumping heart.

Gray caught her hand. 'Wait. Please listen to me. You've

got me all wrong, but I guess that's my own stupid fault. I certainly don't want to own you or just think of you as some pretty object. Look…this isn't coming out the way I wanted it to. The truth is I'd hoped you would come home with me tonight…stay the night with me. At least if you come back to the house I can better explain my feelings to you. What do you say?'

Another leap of hope rocketed through her, but Karen couldn't allow herself to trust it…not when she'd been down that uncertain and painful road with Gray before. 'I don't know…' She shrugged, feeling cold again, and couldn't prevent her voice sounding a little disconsolate.

'I've got an idea.' He opened the front passenger door and held it wide with a flourish. 'Get in and we'll drive down to the beach. We'll stand in the moonlight and watch the waves lapping onto the shore. What do you say?'

Regarding the vital, handsome man issuing the invitation, his haunting grey eyes compelling her like nothing else could, how could she refuse?

Even if things didn't work out she'd always have the memory of him asking her to go to the beach one night to look at the ocean together in the moonlight. Only a man with poetry in his soul could do that.

Shivering again in her inadequately warm jacket, Karen smiled tentatively. 'Okay,' she agreed simply.

They travelled in silence down to the deserted beach, and a strange sense of peace came over Gray that he had never felt before. He could only put it down to the pleasure of Karen's company and the feeling that somehow, by some miracle, everything in his world was beginning to change for the better. It was the most exhilarating thought. For the first time in the longest time hope had found a chink in the fortress he'd built round his feelings in order to protect himself from further hurt, and he was glad it had. Locking the car, he swept his arm firmly round Karen's waist and guided her down to the seashore.

As they walked, their feet sinking a little into the sand, the raw wind whipped at her hair and her warm, musky perfume subtly invaded his senses—not only making his blood slow and heavy in his veins but making him smile, too. As they reached the water's edge Gray's appreciative glance met the stunning vista before him in silent awe. The lapping of the ocean against the moonlit white sand sounded like hushed breath…*the breath of life*, he realised. It was as though life was beckoning to him to live it again as never before. Being here, with this lovely woman who made his heart beat faster every time he saw her, every time he so much as *thought* of her, made him feel intensely alive—almost as if he'd been holed up behind a hundred-foot wall for years but had now been miraculously freed.

'If I were a painter,' Karen said softly beside him, '*this* is the scene I'd most want to paint.'

Turning towards her, Gray curved his mouth in a smile. 'I'll teach you.'

'To paint, you mean?'

As she fastened her big blue eyes on him her eager glance all but made him dissolve. The moonlight bathed her exquisite features in its soft ethereal ray and her incandescent beauty took his breath away. She was utterly ravishing. Gazing into her lovely face, Gray longed to get back to the portrait he'd started and finish it. When it was done it would occupy pride of place in his house…above his bed.

'Would you like to learn?'

'I'd probably be hopeless.'

'Like you're hopeless at singing and playing the guitar, I suppose?' he teased, catching a long strand of her honey-blonde hair and coiling it gently round his fingers.

'I could teach you to play the guitar in return for you teaching me to paint. Can you sing?'

'Not a note. Someone told me once that I had a voice that could shatter a double-glazed window.'

His even white teeth glinted in the moonlight and the mirth in his unreserved grin made Karen yearn to hug him tight and not let him go for a very long time.

'You're cold,' he observed, suddenly serious again. 'Come here.'

Gray pulled her close into his chest and her arms automatically slid round his waist. Resting her cheek over his heart, she briefly closed her eyes to breathe him in. It wasn't just his incredible physicality that she loved, she reflected—though as men went he was pretty compelling—it was the sheer vibrancy and essence of the man, the innate goodness in him that she loved best of all. The goodness he had withheld from the world for too long through grief and guilt.

'I still miss them, you know.'

Realising straight away who he meant, Karen all but held her breath. Behind them the sound of the ocean lapping onto the shore was like mesmerising music.

'I know I never really knew my mother, but somehow there's a lingering impression of her warmth and softness that I can't shake. The memory steals over me sometimes when I'm least expecting it.' The strong arms that surrounded her tightened a little. 'My father never spoke about why she took her own life, so I don't suppose I'll ever know the reason. For a long time I was angry with him for that. I expect he did it to protect me, but at the same time he probably blamed himself. He liked to promote the image that he was as tough as old boots, but underneath he was soft as butter and sentimental, too. He must have missed her like crazy when she went.'

He fell silent. A moment later Karen sensed the shudder

that went through him and, alarmed, glanced up to find the glistening sheen of tears in his eyes.

Stricken by his sorrow, she put her arms round his neck and hugged him hard. 'Oh, Gray...' Reaching up on tiptoe, she planted a tender kiss on his mouth and gently wiped the track of moisture that dampened his cheek with the pad of her thumb. 'It's all right, my darling... They're together again now, and at peace. I'm sure of it.'

Gray's silver moonlit gaze locked with hers. 'That's a comforting thought... And what about Ryan? It must have broken his heart to leave you. Is he at peace, too, Karen?'

Her heart swelled, but she didn't cry. Somewhere locked in time was the ocean of tears that she'd cried for the kind, gentle man who had once been her husband. 'I like to believe he is. God knows he deserves to be.'

'Maybe all the ones we've lost look down on us, silently urging us to live the very best lives we can in their memory?'

'That's so beautiful, Gray.' Laying her palm at the side of his face, Karen smiled gently.

'Perhaps you just bring out the best in me?'

'Maybe... But now that your secret's out you can't ever go back to how you were before,' she told him solemnly.

'What secret?' Stroking his palm down over her hair, Gray stiffened for a moment.

'You act like a lion, but underneath you're just as sentimental and tender as your dad. In truth, you're just a pussycat.'

'A pussycat? That's the most outrageous accusation I've ever heard in my life. Take it back—take it back right now, woman, or you'll be sorry!'

He started tickling her with intent, and Karen could scarce catch her breath for laughing. But then he clasped his hands round her waist and whirled her round and round on the sand, making her utterly and completely dizzy and disorientated.

'Gray, please… Stop right now or I'll be dizzy for the rest of my life!' she begged, even as she laughed.

'Only if you agree to come home with me right now.' Kissing her ear, he came to a sudden standstill.

Out of breath and with her heart racing, Karen didn't hesitate to give him her answer. 'Yes!' She smiled as he returned her carefully to her feet again. 'Yes, I'll come home with you, Gray.' His eyes were languorous with need, she saw, and the realisation thrilled her.

Capturing a handful of her wind-blown hair, he planted a hot hard kiss on her mouth that instantly had her senses clamouring for more.

'Race you to the car,' he taunted, and headed off across the sand like a sprinter.

Laughing again, knowing she didn't have a hope of beating him, Karen chased after him…

When Gray opened the door of the grand old house that was his home, Karen definitely didn't feel like laughing. Straight away she noticed the newly framed paintings lining the high walls, and for a moment was speechless with delight.

Turning to the man at her side—a man who had fallen worryingly silent since they'd left the car—she grabbed his hand and squeezed it. 'You hung the paintings… Gray, that's wonderful!

'I never would have done it if it hadn't been for you,' he answered quietly. 'It was your encouragement and belief in me that did it. You made me face up to a lot of my self-inflicted behaviour, too…my bad habits.' He grinned, looping his arm affectionately round her waist and hugging her to him.

'I think you credit me with far too much. Sooner or later you would have woken up to your true nature as well as your talent, Gray.'

'You think so?'

'I do… But I think sometimes we really do have to hit rock-bottom before we reassess our life. I can't pretend to know what your answer is, but even if it's just to be the wonderful man you are…that's enough.'

'Wonderful, is it?' He brought her hand up to his lips and warmly kissed her fingers. 'That doesn't come close to what I think of you, my bright-eyed girl. But I think it's going to take the rest of the night for me to tell you every superlative that springs to mind.'

'Really…? The rest of the night, you say?' The warmth that flooded Karen at his words extended right down to the edges of her toes. The hope that she'd dared to feel earlier when he'd promised to share his feelings with her returned.

'Really. But first I think we need a drink to warm us up, don't you? What's it to be? Hot chocolate or whiskey?'

'Hot chocolate, I think. I already feel light-headed. But before we get our drinks I want to look at your paintings.'

'Okay. Your wish is my command.'

Hand in hand, they started to walk past the art on the walls together, inspecting it. At the end of the corridor, completely taking them by surprise, Bridie appeared. She had her warm woollen coat on, ready to leave for home. It was way past the time she usually stayed, and Gray's frown was a concerned one.

'Bridie…shouldn't you be home by now? Is anything the matter? It's not Chase?' His stomach rolled over at the mere thought.

Clasping her generous-sized maroon handbag in front of her checked coat, the kind-hearted woman who had cooked and cleaned for him since he'd returned to Ireland, who had put up with his surly moods and dark ways and carried on doing what she could for him regardless, met his anxious gaze with a gentle smile.

'The dog is fine, Mr O'Connell. He's asleep in front of the fire as usual.'

'Then what is it?'

'I was looking at the picture you did of you and your mother—the one that you painted from the photograph your father showed me once. This one.'

She moved towards the painting nearest to where she stood and Gray's heart lurched. Wordlessly—with Karen's hand clasped firmly in his—he found himself standing in front of the lovingly painted portrait of mother and child. At his request the picture-framer had given it his best gilt-edged frame—one embossed with beautifully made golden leaves.

'What about it?'

'She would have been so proud if she'd seen it. "My little man is going to do something great one day," she'd say to everyone. Never had a mother loved her baby as devotedly as your mam loved you, Mr O'Connell...Gray...' Bridie sniffed, her top lip quivering a little.

Gray froze.

'It was herself that she couldn't love,' she continued. 'Your father was always telling her how lovely she was, that she meant the world to him...but she was dogged by this terrible depression that no doctor could help cure. It was pitiful to see the way she got sometimes. We knew it had got bad, but nobody expected her to do what she did. It was an awful shock. She used to go down to the sea all the time, staring out at the horizon as if there was some answer in the waves that could help her. One day she didn't come back. Her poor body was washed up on the shore the next day. When it happened your father wanted to die, too. But he knew he had a child to take care of, and so he devoted himself to working hard on the farm and raising you in a way that would have made your mother proud. I know Paddy never talked about your mother's death with you, Mr O'Connell, and I can't say those of us who knew him agreed with that. We all believed he should have told you the truth long ago, but there...' The housekeeper shook her head sadly. 'He did his best, God rest him. When I saw the picture I realised how much you must still think about her, and I just felt it was right to tell you. I hope you won't hold it against me?'

Breaking out of the painful trance that had taken him prisoner, Gray cleared his throat and forced a smile. 'Of course I don't hold it against you, Bridie.' He let go of Karen's hand, stepping forward to embrace the older woman in a fierce hug. 'Thank you—thank you for telling me. But you'd better get yourself off home now. It's late. I'll see you on Monday morning as usual, okay?'

When the front door had closed behind the housekeeper, Gray dropped his hands to his hips and stared blankly down at the floor.

'Gray?' Moving closer, Karen reached for his hand but, distracted, he turned away and headed for the staircase.

'Just give me a few minutes, will you?' In the midst of the fog of pain that engulfed him he prayed she would understand.

'Of course.' Her reply was softly compassionate...

CHAPTER ELEVEN

HALF an hour passed and Gray still hadn't reappeared. Sitting on the sofa, with Chase's great fawn head in her lap, Karen grew increasingly anxious about his state of mind. She was also getting cold in that big lonely room, but too wrapped up in her concern for Gray to stoke the fire.

Unable to sit and wait any longer, she spoke softly to Chase, telling him to stay. Even before she reached the door the Great Dane had made his way back to the dying fire in the grate and with a great sigh lay down in front of it.

Locating the perfectly tidied kitchen, with its gleaming iron range, meticulously swept stone-flagged floor and beautiful Irish dresser lined with rows of delicate white and patterned crockery, Karen hunted down a saucepan, boiled some milk, and made two mugs of hot chocolate. The rain that lashed rhythmically at the windows was a haunting accompaniment as she worked.

Bridie's story about Gray's mother had been heartrending. She wondered how the housekeeper had borne the truth for so long without being tempted to tell him before. All Karen could think was that she must have respected his father very highly to keep it a secret. If Gray hadn't displayed the portrait of his mother would he ever have found out what happened? She could only imagine the legacy of sorrow he'd had to live with, knowing his mother had taken her own life.

Suddenly impatient to be with him again, she gave the hot drinks a final stir and then, with her heart in her mouth, climbed the great winding staircase to the first floor. She was hoping she'd find Gray without having to search behind every door, and silently prayed that he hadn't descended into so deep a despair that she wouldn't be able to reach him. It was obvious that Bridie's words had profoundly affected him, and now she longed for the opportunity to talk and offer solace.

In the end, Karen didn't have to search very far to find him.

At the end of the first-floor corridor a door was ajar. When she reached it she softly called out his name. Receiving no answer, she nudged the door wider with her elbow and went inside. In the impressive high-ceilinged room, with its tasteful muted decoration and spare antique furniture, Gray was seated on a huge carved bed with his back to her, his dark head bowed, his hands resting on his jean-clad thighs. She felt such a powerful rush of love for him that for a moment she was literally struck dumb.

Leaving the mugs of chocolate on the nearest cherrywood bedside cabinet, Karen moved quietly round to the still silent man. Sucking in a nervous breath, she reached out to lay her hand on his hard-muscled shoulder. 'I'm so sorry, Gray. I'm so sorry about your mother… It must have been so hard for you and your dad to live without her. But maybe now that you know the truth about why she did what she did it might help you to understand that it was out of anyone's hands? No one was to blame.'

Slowly he raised his head and looked at her. The raw, unfettered glance he gave her was shocking and said so much more than words. For a moment her limbs felt frozen and she couldn't move. Then, as if a switch had been flicked, Karen's blood turned into a wild river of molten need that suspended everything. Only the desire to comfort and help him in any way that she could remained.

'I've been haunted for a long time about why she would do it…why I wasn't enough to make her stay.'

'Oh, Gray. It wasn't that you weren't enough—there was nothing you did wrong. How could you have? You were just a beautiful innocent little boy, and your mother was suffering from depression. It can be the most terrible illness.'

She put her arms round him to give him a warm, sympathetic hug, but suddenly the tenor of that hug turned into something much more compelling. Karen sensed Gray tense, then breathe out on a ragged sigh. Her heart pumping wildly, she suddenly found herself tipped into his lap, and with his hands placed either side of her face his lips ravished her mouth with the kind of primal urgency and demand that made her feel as if she was at the epicentre of a sensual hurricane.

As he groaned into her mouth his teeth clashed against hers, his scalding velvet tongue mimicking the kind of unbridled sex that made her snatch at her breath. His heat burned her all the way down to her soul. Momentarily lifting his head, he stared intensely into her eyes and his gaze transmitted everything—every emotion, every feeling he had ever felt. If Karen hadn't already been sitting on Gray's lap she would have been knocked off her feet by that shockingly frank glance.

But she barely had time to register what lay in those depths before she found herself on her back, her mind spinning and her blood throbbing heavily through her veins as his hands urgently helped her part with her clothes. Removing the leather jacket he was still wearing, he pulled his sweater and tee shirt over his head, jettisoned them carelessly behind him, then unzipped his jeans. Roughly tugging at the sides of Karen's black silk panties, he yanked them down over her slender thighs and plunged himself deep inside her.

Shutting her eyes, she registered the shock of their passionate union with an unrestrained broken cry—a feral sound that was punched from her lungs and didn't hide her pleasure or her need. Driving her fingers hungrily through the silken mass of his ebony hair, she raised her legs up to clasp his hard, lean hips and take him even deeper. His mouth descended on each breast in turn—first to suckle, then to nip—spearing ecstatic arrows of explosive sensation straight to her womb. The volcanic fever that was already close to erupting inside her clung precariously to the heady precipice of her desire. Then, as Gray rocked her hard, it *did* erupt.

As Karen soared dizzyingly into the erotic sensual stratosphere that he took her to she held on to his arms, her fingernails biting helplessly into the iron-hard biceps that surrounded her. The lean, tight hips above her vigorously slammed against hers as he thrust again and again, then went powerfully still, releasing a throaty groan of ecstatic release that echoed in her ears even as she dazedly realised that he'd knowingly spilled his seed inside her.

Now her heart *did* drum hard.

He dropped his head against her breasts, and as well as the slightly roughened scrape of his unshaven jaw she sensed the warm leakage of moisture from his eyes. She knew Gray was shedding silent, soul-deep tears for the family he had so tragically lost. Her fingers tunnelled softly through his silken hair and gently massaged his scalp. Their wild sexual coupling had been a way to help him purge some of his pain, she realised. Now that the storm had passed he must be feeling empty and raw.

Powerful emotion like that had a way of scraping your insides clean, Karen knew. She'd experienced it many times in the days and months following Ryan's death.

Lifting himself away from her, Gray smiled ruefully down, wiping his hand roughly across his face to remove the traces of his distress before moving to her side and firmly enfolding her in his arms.

'I love you,' he said simply.

The huskily voiced declaration stopped her world in its tracks. When the shockwaves started to ebb, she laid her hand over his heart and lifted her gaze to his.

'I love you, too, Gray,' she admitted softly, without reservation. He went still. 'Gray?' she prompted nervously.

'I've never felt like this about anyone before…never felt that I would gladly surrender everything I have, give away everything I owned, just to be with a woman. But that's how I feel when I'm with you, Karen. At first I thought it was some crazy obsession that had taken hold of me, but now I know for sure that it's love. It was love all along, if I'm honest. From the first moment you angrily tore into me in the woods. I couldn't believe it. You were just a slip of a thing, and yet you didn't hesitate to quite rightly put me in my place. Do you know how much it scares me to want and need you so much?'

He caught her hand and kissed the delicate skin across her knuckles. Her gaze tenderly examined his. 'Why does it scare you to love me?'

'I don't want to lose you.'

As he touched his palm to her cheek his expression had never been so starkly vulnerable, and Karen knew he must be mulling over the tragic losses that had made him wary of giving his heart to anyone ever again.

'You won't lose me, Gray. I mean to stay with you for a very long time. I never thought I'd ever want to be with another man after I lost Ryan…but I was wrong. Even though you were gruff and defensive when we first met—yes, and bossy and angry, too—I knew that wasn't the real you. I'm glad I stayed around to find out the truth.'

'I behaved the way I did because I was lost, Karen. Utterly lost… That is until I met you. I'd made my fortune, but my personal life was a train hurtling towards a cliff-edge. I'd lost faith in everything…didn't see the point in aiming for anything ever again. I couldn't even enjoy my wealth because I despised what I'd done to make it, and I wore my rage and disappointment in myself and the world like a shield.'

'I know it must have been agony for you to hear it, but did it help when Bridie told you about your mother? About her illness, I mean?'

The dark-lashed silvery eyes closed briefly. 'I suppose it brought an end to my wild imaginings that my father might have somehow driven her to end her life. It's a relief to find out the truth at last and get some closure, I suppose. And to know that my dad was the solidly loyal man I always secretly believed him to be. But just the mere thought of her standing there on the beach alone, looking out to sea…it still tears me up.'

'I know, my darling, but you're strong…much stronger than you think you are. And whenever you get down about the past in future I'll be there to listen if you want to talk, and to help you in any way that I can. You won't be alone any more.'

'And I'll do the same for you, sweetheart. You've had a hell of a tough journey, too. I haven't forgotten that. It pains me to ask you, but do you still miss him? Ryan, I mean?'

Karen didn't know the precise moment when missing him had turned into poignant acceptance that he was gone and the realisation that she must build a new life for herself, but somehow that was what had happened. Maybe it wouldn't have happened so soon if she hadn't fallen in love with Gray, but she thanked God that she had.

Looking straight into his worried glance now, she had no reservation in speaking to him from the heart. 'I'll never forget him, but I don't miss him any more…no. And he was the kind of man who would want me to find love again…to build a new life with someone who really cared about me and who I cared for. To tell you the truth, music was the main passion we shared… Ryan wasn't able to love me in the way that you do, Gray.' She felt her blood grow hot at the frank admission. 'But what happened to both of us is in the past. We can't live the rest of our lives in fear of bad things happening again, because living in fear means that we can't ever trust that things can get better—and I honestly believe that they can.'

'As long as you know that you're going to have to make an honest man of me now—because I won't live in sin, you know. I do have morals to uphold.'

'Morals, my—'

'Tut-tut… That's not the kind of response I expect from a lady,' he teased.

Karen grinned, feeling a joyous surge of hope and delight pulse through her. 'Are you certain that you want to be with me, Gray?' she asked, momentary doubt making her anxious.

Stroking her hair, Gray sighed deeply. 'I don't think I've ever felt so certain about the rightness of a thing in my life,' he admitted thoughtfully. 'I'd be an absolute fool if I were to let you go, Karen Ford. I'm many things…uptight, morose, and—yes—too prone to giving in to my temper sometimes. But I'm no fool.'

Rising to her knees, her honey-gold hair spilling wildly across her shoulders, Karen stared in wonder down into the darkly handsome face with the haunting silvery eyes she had so come to love, and inside her chest her heart skipped a beat.

'What did you mean by you won't live in sin?'

'What do you think I meant?' His hands were guiding her over him as he talked, bringing the backs of her slender thighs down flat across his more softly hirsute limbs. She quickly discovered that he was heavily aroused again, and her blood began to thrum as he eased his way inside her, his hands possessively enfolding her hips as he did so.

'I mean that I want to marry you, my gorgeous girl… Will you have me as your husband?'

'Yes, Gray…I will!'

Eagerly she bent her head to meet his lips in a passionately tender kiss, and although their loving was no less intense it was also infused with the joy and wonder of finding each other after all the heartache and pain they had endured before they'd met—and gratitude, too, that they'd both been given this second chance.

Later, lying in the cavernous bed beside Karen as she slept, her lovely golden hair spread out on the pillow beneath her, Gray deliberately elected to stay awake. It was extraordinarily peaceful, lying there with the sound of the rain glancing off the windows, and he just wanted to savour these precious moments when he was on the brink of joining the land of the living again. He'd stay awake all night if he had to, just to experience the joy of watching the woman next to him, knowing that she'd agreed to be his wife and wouldn't be saying goodbye as he had once feared she might. No more would he ask himself what he'd done to deserve such good fortune he vowed. Instead he resolved simply to be grateful and count his blessings.

Before his mother had become so ill had she and his father felt this way about each other? Gray wondered. As if nothing could add to their quota of joy because they had each other? Had his father lain in bed beside his mother, as his son was doing now with Karen, and thought how beautiful and perfect she was and what a blessed miracle it would be were they to have a child together?

A jolt went through his heart. He hadn't protected Karen when he'd so passionately made love to her earlier, and she hadn't mentioned it. *Would she mind if she fell pregnant*? he worried. Because suddenly he knew that he desperately longed for children of his own. To have the chance to be a father...a *good* father...and pass on some of the bravery and devotion that his own father had shown him—despite Paddy's ultimate disappointment that Gray hadn't followed in his footsteps with the farm. That would be something he could really be proud of.

He sighed and stretched, turning back to observe what looked to be an intriguing little smile playing on his lover's lips as she slept. She'd lost that air of sadness and vulnerability she'd had when they first met, Gray realised, and for that he was hugely grateful. He almost couldn't bear the thought of her being unhappy—not even for a moment. Now, as he studied her, he didn't think that she would mind carrying his baby. And if she wanted to pursue her singing career then he would make sure that she had the chance to do that, too. His wife-to-be deserved everything her beautiful heart desired. He'd never known a woman who had so much love to give. There would be more than enough for them all—him and their children.

Settling down at last, he wrapped her in his arms and willingly surrendered to sleep...

Karen was pacing the floor again, one hand pressed into the small of her back to try and ease the ache that had started that morning and still hadn't subsided, even though it was now late afternoon. It had obviously crossed her mind that it might be the onset of labour, but as the pain hadn't exactly intensified or grown worse she had her doubts. No. It was simply that she was heavily pregnant, felt as if she was about to pop, and wouldn't sit down and rest.

Much to her friend Liz's concern, she wouldn't heed any of the advice that either her or the full-time maternity nurse/

midwife that Gray had hired to stay with them regularly offered.

Now Margaret—the plump but agile nurse—had gone to make them all tea, and Karen anxiously watched the clock, hoping that her husband would get home soon from his trip to Dublin. If she did go into labour any time soon, she wanted him there.

He'd gone there yesterday, to make a guest appearance at the gallery that was displaying his work, and because of her heavily pregnant state she hadn't been able to accompany him. The gallery was a highly prestigious one, and she'd told him to mind his p's and q's and not get shirty with anybody. She knew when Gray was tense his patience was apt to get a little short. It was quite likely that he would be tense now, as Karen had just discovered that Margaret had phoned him on his mobile around lunchtime, when he'd been on the road driving home, to helpfully inform him that his wife was showing definite signs of going into labour any time now, and that he should get home sooner rather than later.

'Come and sit down, you stubborn woman.'

Suddenly Liz was there beside her again, her expression concerned, but annoyed, too. The women had become the best of friends over the past year, and Karen sensed that she understood her more than any other female she'd ever known. The enterprising café owner had recently become engaged to the lovely Jorge, and frequent visits to Karen and Gray's beautifully refurbished home were becoming quite a feature, so that Liz could eagerly discuss her plans for their wedding in June.

Allowing the other woman to lead her to a sumptuous couch, not far from the crackling fire in the elegantly stunning Adam fireplace, Karen finally gave in and sat down. Even as she accepted a welcome cup of tea from Margaret she heard Gray's key in the door—the door that was near slammed off its hinges as her husband strode anxiously into the drawing room, his coat undone and its shoulders covered in a melting dusting of icy November rain. Her heart quickening—as it always did whenever he was near—Karen smiled up at him, not hiding her relief that he'd returned.

'You always bring the rain,' she joked. 'Lucky for me that rain is one of my favourite things.'

His handsome face serious, Gray ignored the remark and dropped down in front of her as the nurse and Liz helpfully left the room. Removing the cup and saucer she was holding, he left it on a small side table to take her hands in his and hold them.

'Are you all right? You're not in labour yet? I panicked when Margaret phoned me.'

'I wish she hadn't done that, but she was only thinking of me. She knows how much I want you to be there. I hope you didn't drive too fast?'

'I wouldn't take a foolish risk like that, and thankfully the roads were clear all the way home. So, tell me, has anything started yet?'

'No. I'm not in labour yet—and apart from feeling a little like a floundering whale I'm well and happy.'

'That's my girl.'

He kissed her then, and Karen tasted the rain and the wind on the sculpted lips that she so adored. For a moment she wished that she could go down to the ocean with him, so that she could taste the scent of the sea on them too. But right now she would settle for lying down beside him in their bed and having him hold her. *She'd never told him how afraid she was of giving birth…how terrified she was that something might go wrong.* But in truth she was more scared about the effect such an event might have on him, rather than on herself.

'How did it go at the reception? I'll bet the handsome

guest artist had all the well-heeled Dublin ladies swooning over him!'

'If he did,' Gray replied dryly, 'he didn't notice, because his mind was on his beautiful wife back at home, about to go into labour with their first child any time now. Besides, my female admirers are serious connoisseurs of art, I'll have you know. Not the type of women who swoon easily.'

'Unless they've all got white sticks, I don't believe that for a second. Anyway, I don't think it's going to happen today, my love. Me going into labour, I mean.' Lightly tracing his clean-cut jaw, already showing signs of a five o'clock shadow because he was so dark, Karen shrugged. 'Things will probably kick off tomorrow.'

'In that case you'd better just rest and take things easy. No doubt you've been driving poor Margaret and Liz crazy, ignoring their advice to sit down. Right, then.' He got to his feet and slipped his black cashmere coat from his shoulders. 'I'm going to see if one of them will take pity on your poor husband and make me a cup of coffee.'

'They'll probably fight over the chance. By the way—did I tell you how proud I am of you? Now everyone who sees your paintings will know what a great talent you are. Anyway, I— *Ohh*...' A breathtaking, sharp slash of pain reverberated through Karen's insides.

Immediately Gray dropped down in front of her again, touching his palm concernedly to her cheek.

'Karen?'

'I'm okay,' she breathed, starting to smile. A second, even more acute pain froze the expression on her face.

If this was the onset of labour wasn't there supposed to be a longer interval between each contraction? she thought. She sent up a swift prayer that everything would go well, refusing to believe that disaster would strike at the eleventh hour and rob them of their longed-for dream of a healthy child.

'You'd better get Margaret.' She grimaced as the pain started to subside, already in anxious anticipation of the next one.

'Everything's going to be fine, I promise. I don't want you to worry,' Gray soothed her. 'I'm going to be with you every step of the way, remember?'

Planting a loving kiss at the corner of her mouth, he shot up and hurried into the kitchen, calling out for the nurse as he went...

His wife's labour had been intense and fast—too fast to make it to the hospital, even. Instead, Karen had given birth to their beautiful baby son at home.

Gray had thanked God more than once that he'd hired a midwife to stay at the house with them, to be on hand in case of just such an eventuality, despite the teasing he had suffered for going to such measures. Now, as he cradled his son— Padraic William, as he and Karen had named him: Padraic after Gray's father and William after hers—he couldn't stop inspecting the awesome perfection of the infant swaddled in his soft woollen blanket. Right now his baby son had a thatch of silky black hair and dark blue eyes, and if that stunning combination should remain then he would be a heartbreaker for sure.

A tumult of feelings swamped him as Gray sat there in the armchair by the bed, his elated gaze vying between looking at Karen—still breathtakingly lovely, even after the drama of her unexpectedly quick and intense labour—and his precious baby son. And as he sat there, happier and more content than he had ever felt in his life, he could almost be persuaded that he sensed the loving spirits of his parents come around him and smile lovingly down at him and his beautiful new family, as if giving them their blessing.

'What are you smiling about, hmm?' Leaning towards

him from the bed, Karen was stroking her fingers tenderly down Gray's forearm, her bright blue eyes looking tired but happy.

'What do you think I'm smiling about, you clever, beautiful girl? I'm the luckiest man in the world and I can't quite believe it.'

'Then you'd better believe it, Gray O'Connell, because I'm sure I didn't imagine the agony I went through to present you with your son!'

That wiped his next thought clean out of his head, and he remembered his wife's face, contorted with pain, and the angry words flung at him at the height of her agony. 'Was it very bad?' he asked quietly, his voice slightly gruff with emotion.

She pushed back his unruly hair with her fingers and smiled lovingly. 'There was nothing bad about it, my love. I was only teasing. Every ounce of discomfort was more than worth it to produce our lovely little man. He's adorable, isn't he?' She moved her hand to let it rest lovingly on the baby's head.

'He is. Absolutely adorable.'

'And so is his father,' Karen added, her blue eyes now moist with tears.

'Don't cry, sweetheart, or you'll have me bawling my eyes out, too—and that's not a good look for a man with a reputation like mine for being mysterious and forbidding. By the way, I've got a gift for you.'

Clutching the sleeping baby securely to his chest, Gray reached into his trouser pocket for the envelope he'd put there for safekeeping earlier. It was slightly crumpled as he handed it to her, and his accompanying grin was rueful.

'I should have made a better presentation of it than that… tied it up with a big pink bow, or something…but I'm afraid I'm not very good at that sort of thing.'

'You may not be good at tying big pink bows, but there's

a long list of other things that you *are* good at. You shouldn't have bought me another gift. I've already got everything I could possibly want—and I mean you and little Padraic.'

When she carefully tore open the envelope, lifted out the officially printed sheet of paper inside and scanned the written contents, Karen shook her head and stared at Gray in disbelief. 'You're giving me your father's cottage and the fifty acres of land surrounding it? Oh, Gray! It's too much—it's far too generous.'

'No, it's not. Besides, you more than deserve it—and you love that place. It's just a small gesture from me, to thank you for all the joy and happiness you've brought me. You can renovate or rebuild, and I thought you might like to use some of the land to build your own recording studio on. I've already spoken to a specialist architect, and as soon as you're feeling up to it we can drive over there and you can start making plans for what you'd like. I know how important your music is to you, my love.'

'Gray O'Connell?'

'Yes, Mrs O'Connell?'

'I want you to bring our baby and get into bed beside me right now!'

'If I must.' With a theatrical waggle of his eyebrows, Gray got to his feet and did exactly as his wife ordered…

JUNE 2011
HARDBACK TITLES

ROMANCE

Passion and the Prince	Penny Jordan
For Duty's Sake	Lucy Monroe
Alessandro's Prize	Helen Bianchin
Mr and Mischief	Kate Hewitt
Wife in the Shadows	Sara Craven
The Brooding Stranger	Maggie Cox
An Inconvenient Obsession	Natasha Tate
The Girl He Never Noticed	Lindsay Armstrong
The Privileged and the Damned	Kimberly Lang
The Big Bad Boss	Susan Stephens
Her Desert Prince	Rebecca Winters
A Family for the Rugged Rancher	Donna Alward
The Boss's Surprise Son	Teresa Carpenter
Soldier on Her Doorstep	Soraya Lane
Ordinary Girl in a Tiara	Jessica Hart
Tempted by Trouble	Liz Fielding
Flirting with the Society Doctor	Janice Lynn
When One Night Isn't Enough	Wendy S Marcus

HISTORICAL

Ravished by the Rake	Louise Allen
The Rake of Hollowhurst Castle	Elizabeth Beacon
Bought for the Harem	Anne Herries
Slave Princess	Juliet Landon

MEDICAL™

Melting the Argentine Doctor's Heart	Meredith Webber
Small Town Marriage Miracle	Jennifer Taylor
St Piran's: Prince on the Children's Ward	Sarah Morgan
Harry St Clair: Rogue or Doctor?	Fiona McArthur

JUNE 2011
LARGE PRINT TITLES

ROMANCE

Flora's Defiance	Lynne Graham
The Reluctant Duke	Carole Mortimer
The Wedding Charade	Melanie Milburne
The Devil Wears Kolovsky	Carol Marinelli
The Nanny and the CEO	Rebecca Winters
Friends to Forever	Nikki Logan
Three Weddings and a Baby	Fiona Harper
The Last Summer of Being Single	Nina Harrington

HISTORICAL

Lady Arabella's Scandalous Marriage	Carole Mortimer
Dangerous Lord, Seductive Miss	Mary Brendan
Bound to the Barbarian	Carol Townend
The Shy Duchess	Amanda McCabe

MEDICAL™

St Piran's: The Wedding of The Year	Caroline Anderson
St Piran's: Rescuing Pregnant Cinderella	Carol Marinelli
A Christmas Knight	Kate Hardy
The Nurse Who Saved Christmas	Janice Lynn
The Midwife's Christmas Miracle	Jennifer Taylor
The Doctor's Society Sweetheart	Lucy Clark

JULY 2011
HARDBACK TITLES

ROMANCE

The Marriage Betrayal	Lynne Graham
The Ice Prince	Sandra Marton
Doukakis's Apprentice	Sarah Morgan
Surrender to the Past	Carole Mortimer
Heart of the Desert	Carol Marinelli
Reckless Night in Rio	Jennie Lucas
Her Impossible Boss	Cathy Williams
The Replacement Wife	Caitlin Crews
Dating and Other Dangers	Natalie Anderson
The S Before Ex	Mira Lyn Kelly
Her Outback Commander	Margaret Way
A Kiss to Seal the Deal	Nikki Logan
Baby on the Ranch	Susan Meier
The Army Ranger's Return	Soraya Lane
Girl in a Vintage Dress	Nicola Marsh
Rapunzel in New York	Nikki Logan
The Doctor & the Runaway Heiress	Marion Lennox
The Surgeon She Never Forgot	Melanie Milburne

HISTORICAL

Seduced by the Scoundrel	Louise Allen
Unmasking the Duke's Mistress	Margaret McPhee
To Catch a Husband…	Sarah Mallory
The Highlander's Redemption	Marguerite Kaye

MEDICAL™

The Playboy of Harley Street	Anne Fraser
Doctor on the Red Carpet	Anne Fraser
Just One Last Night...	Amy Andrews
Suddenly Single Sophie	Leonie Knight

JULY 2011
LARGE PRINT TITLES

ROMANCE

A Stormy Spanish Summer — Penny Jordan
Taming the Last St Claire — Carole Mortimer
Not a Marrying Man — Miranda Lee
The Far Side of Paradise — Robyn Donald
The Baby Swap Miracle — Caroline Anderson
Expecting Royal Twins! — Melissa McClone
To Dance with a Prince — Cara Colter
Molly Cooper's Dream Date — Barbara Hannay

HISTORICAL

Lady Folbroke's Delicious Deception — Christine Merrill
Breaking the Governess's Rules — Michelle Styles
Her Dark and Dangerous Lord — Anne Herries
How To Marry a Rake — Deb Marlowe

MEDICAL™

Sheikh, Children's Doctor...Husband — Meredith Webber
Six-Week Marriage Miracle — Jessica Matthews
Rescued by the Dreamy Doc — Amy Andrews
Navy Officer to Family Man — Emily Forbes
St Piran's: Italian Surgeon, Forbidden Bride — Margaret McDonagh
The Baby Who Stole the Doctor's Heart — Dianne Drake